THE VEGETABLE

TO
KATHERINE TIGHE AND EDMUND WILSON, Jr.
WHO DELETED MANY ABSURDITIES
FROM MY FIRST TWO NOVELS I RECOMMEND
THE ABSURDITIES SET DOWN HERE

BY F. SCOTT FITZGERALD

NOVELS

THE LAST TYCOON *(unfinished)*
  with a foreword by Edmund Wilson and notes by the author
TENDER IS THE NIGHT
THE GREAT GATSBY
THE BEAUTIFUL AND DAMNED
THIS SIDE OF PARADISE

STORIES

BITS OF PARADISE
  uncollected stories by Scott and Zelda Fitzgerald
THE BASIL AND JOSEPHINE STORIES
  edited with an introduction by Jackson R. Bryer and John Kuehl
THE PAT HOBBY STORIES
  with an introduction by Arnold Gingrich
TAPS AT REVEILLE
SIX TALES OF THE JAZZ AGE AND OTHER STORIES
  with an introduction by Frances Fitzgerald Smith
FLAPPERS AND PHILOSOPHERS
  with an introduction by Arthur Mizener
THE STORIES OF F. SCOTT FITZGERALD
  a selection of 28 stories, with an introduction by Malcolm Cowley
BABYLON REVISITED AND OTHER STORIES

STORIES AND ESSAYS

AFTERNOON OF AN AUTHOR
  with an introduction and notes by Arthur Mizener
THE FITZGERALD READER
  with an introduction by Arthur Mizener

LETTERS

THE LETTERS OF F. SCOTT FITZGERALD
  with an introduction by Andrew Turnbull
LETTERS TO HIS DAUGHTER
  with an introduction by Frances Fitzgerald Smith
DEAR SCOTT/DEAR MAX
  edited by John Kuehl and Jackson Bryer

AND A COMEDY

THE VEGETABLE
  with an introduction by Charles Scribner III

THE VEGETABLE

or

from President to postman

By

F. SCOTT FITZGERALD

A new edition with unpublished scenes and corrections and an introduction by Charles Scribner III

"Any man who doesn't want to get on in the world, to make a million dollars, and maybe even park his toothbrush in the White House, hasn't got as much to him as a good dog has—he's nothing more or less than a vegetable."
— *From a Current Magazine.*

CHARLES SCRIBNER'S SONS   NEW YORK

Acknowledgments

The publishers wish to thank Mrs. Elena Wilson and the Princeton University Library for permission to quote from Edmund Wilson's letter to Fitzgerald (26 May 1922), which will appear in the forthcoming book, *Edmund Wilson: Letters on Literature and Politics* (Farrar, Straus and Giroux, Inc., © 1976 Elena Wilson).

We also wish to express our gratitude to the Princeton University Library for its characteristic helpfulness.

Finally, our special thanks to Alexander Clark, Matthew J. Bruccoli, and Edward J. Milne, Jr., for their assistance and advice.

copyright 1923 Charles Scribner's Sons
Introduction copyright © 1976 Charles Scribner's Sons
Appendices copyright © 1976 Frances Scott Fitzgerald Smith

Library of Congress Cataloging in Publication Data

Fitzgerald, Francis Scott Key, 1896-1940.
    The vegetable.
    I. Title.
PS3511.I9V4   1976   812'.5'2   76-2633
ISBN 0-684-14622-3 (cloth)
ISBN 0-684-14623-1 (paper)

1 3 5 7 9 11 13 15 17 19 C/C 20 18 16 14 12 10 8 6 4 2
1 3 5 7 9 11 13 15 17 19 C/P 20 18 16 14 12 10 8 6 4 2

Printed in the United States of America

Introduction

Among the published works of Scott Fitzgerald, *The Vegetable* stands out as something of a curiosity. As the author's only published full-length play, it represents his one attempt to establish himself as a successful playwright. It also represents Fitzgerald's brief excursion into the realm of political satire. In *The Vegetable* an ordinary railroad clerk, Jerry Frost, gets drunk on the eve of Warren Harding's nomination and suddenly finds himself and his entire family in the White House. The consequences are, of course, disastrous, but fortunately Jerry is able to escape them by simply waking up. Much relieved, he can finally fulfill his true calling: to be a postman. Although the play was a failure and Fitzgerald quickly returned to writing short stories and novels, this little-known work deserves to be made available to Fitzgerald's public. Because of its possible interest to students, the publishers have also decided to add appendices, which include scenes cut from the manuscript during the author's many revisions as well as final "corrections and addenda" for the acting script. If, on the one hand, these documents suggest some of Fitzgerald's difficulty and uncertainty in writing for the stage, on the other they clearly reflect the amount of care and craftsmanship that went into this venture.

As a boy, Fitzgerald had a special love for the theater and enjoyed a precocious success as a playwright and impresario. At fourteen, he presented *The Girl from "Lazy J"* at an organizational meeting of the Elizabethan Dramatic Club of St. Paul, Minnesota. As he wrote in his scrapbook, his "head was turned," and the next year the club produced his second drama, *The Captured Shadow,* as a benefit performance for the Baby Welfare Association. Fitzgerald himself played the "Shadow," and later in his scrapbook he wrote, "Enter Success!" This was followed the next summer by a two-act melodrama, *The Coward,* about a reluctant Confederate soldier. According to one reviewer, it, too, was a "decided success." This was just before Fitzgerald's departure for Princeton, but it was not his final production for the club. The summer following his freshman year, he returned to St. Paul and wrote a comedy, *Assorted Spirits,* in which he also acted and served as stage manager. His final performance was unexpectedly memorable, for at one point during the show a fuse blew and there followed an explosion and sudden darkness. But the seasoned actor seized his cue and proceeded to calm the audience with an improvised monologue.

During the academic year, Fitzgerald had become active in the Princeton Triangle Club, which annually produced an original musical comedy. The 1914-15 show, *Fie! Fie! Fi-Fi!,* owed its plot and lyrics to Fitzgerald. In fact, the very notion of a sustained plot tying together the musical numbers was considered a real innovation and the *Louisville Post* proclaimed that Fitzgerald "could take his place right now with the brightest writers of witty lyrics in America." And, to be sure, he continued to write the lyrics for the next two Triangle productions: *The Evil Eye* (1915-16) and *Safety First* (1916-17). In addition, he published in the *Nassau Literary Magazine* a one-act play, *The Débutante,* which would eventually become a chapter in his first novel, *This Side of Paradise.* Though one critic felt that it was "somewhat far-fetched" (an understandable tendency in a Triangle writer), it was praised as "a devastating skit on the foibles of young femininity."

How was Fitzgerald rated by his college contemporaries? In the graduating class poll, he received six votes as their favorite dramatist (Shakespeare received sixty-one and Shaw twenty-nine)—not a bad start. But after Princeton his theatrical career gave way to the ambition of becoming a serious and successful novelist. Yet, his love for scriptwriting was never wholly suppressed, for in his first two novels—*This Side of Paradise* and *The Beautiful and Damned*—several episodes were set as dramatic dialogues complete with stage directions. And two "short stories" for *The Smart Set* magazine were conceived and published as one-act plays: "Porcelain and Pink" and "Mr. Icky" (in *Tales of the Jazz Age,* 1922).

Finally, having published a novel and a collection of short stories *(Flappers and Philosophers,* 1920), Fitzgerald turned his eyes toward Broadway and in the late fall of 1921 wrote to his agent, Harold Ober, "I am conceiving a play which is to make my fortune," adding in a subsequent letter that it "is the funniest ever written." Then, with no less self-confidence, he wrote to his editor at

Scribners, Maxwell Perkins, that he was at work on "an awfully funny play that's going to make me rich forever." From the very start, Fitzgerald viewed the play as something to guarantee his fortune, if not fame as well. On the day before publication of *The Beautiful and Damned,* he wrote to Ober that he was sending him the first draft of the play (which had as yet no title) to be placed with a producer. His opinion of it was still high, but he clearly foresaw the revisions that lay ahead: "I should not, I suppose I should say now, want to collaborate with anyone else in a revision of this. I'm willing to revise it myself with advice from whomsoever they should designate—but I feel that Acts I and III are probably the best pieces of dramatic comedy written in English in the last 5 years and I wouldn't let them go entirely out of my possession nor permit the addition of another name to the authorship of the play."

That was in March. By May he had revised the script, and his former college companion Edmund Wilson was trying to place it with the Theatre Guild. In a long and very revealing letter of 26 May 1922, Wilson offered much praise and suggested structural changes (see Appendix I):

So far as I am concerned, I think it is one of the best things you ever wrote. I have read only the first version—I didn't take time to read the second because the Theater Guild insisted that they were in a great hurry about it—so won't criticize it now at length. I thought the millionaire episode—except the first scene—a little weak and the last act too palpably padded. As for the battle scene, it was fine and you made a great mistake to have allowed them to kid you into removing it. The Guild thinks so too and have expressed disappointment that it isn't in the revised version—so, if they decide to take it, I think you ought to put it back. I should suggest that you make the White House and Battle the second act and the millionaire and postman the third: this would do away with the necessity of stalling along at the beginning of the postman scene simply in order to make it into a whole act.—As I say, I think that the play as a whole is marvellous—no doubt, the best American comedy ever written. I think you have a much better grasp on your subject than you usually have—you know what end and point you are working for, as isn't always the case with you.... I think you have a great gift for comic dialogue—even though you never can resist a stupid gag—and should go on writing plays.... By the way, the great question is, have you read James Joyce's *Ulysses?* Because if you haven't, the resemblances between the drunken visions scene in it and your scene in the White House must take its place as one of the great coincidences of literature.

(It was, in fact, a coincidence.) Soon afterwards, the Guild turned down the play, but Wilson told Fitzgerald that he ought to have it published even before it was accepted for production.

Fitzgerald then set out to revise a second time and in July wrote to Perkins, "At present I'm working on my

play—the same one. . . . Bunny Wilson says that it's without a doubt the best American comedy to date (that's just
between you and me)." By August, it had finally been
given a title, *Gabriel's Trombone,* an allusion to a scene,
later cut from the script (Appendix I), in which the
imminent Apocalypse is predicted by Jerry's senile father,
a Last Judgment heralded in tones familiar to the Jazz Age.

> *Dada:* The world is coming to an end. The last judg-
> ment is at hand. Gabriel's Trump will blow
> one week from today just at this hour.
> *Fish:* What's a trump?
> *Doris:* It's something like a trombone, only not so
> good.

Fitzgerald asked Perkins if *Scribner's Magazine* would
be interested in serializing it, "that is, of course, on condition that it is to be produced this fall." Perkins replied that
he was "mightily interested," adding that "it would be
most unusual if we should publish a play in *Scribner's,* but
we have no rule against it and would like to consider the
possibility." In the meantime, no producer was found and
Fitzgerald continued to revise. By December, the manuscript was in Perkins's hands, now reworked for the third
time, and it bore a new, far simpler title: *Frost.* Perkins
wrote a lengthy and extremely perceptive critique, which
not only articulated the central theme of the satire but
also suggested further revisions:

COMMENT ON "FROST"

(To save space I've omitted most of the "I thinks,"
"It seems to mes," and "I may be wrong buts": they
should, however, be understood)

I've read your play three times and I think more highly of its possibilities on the third reading than ever before;—but I am also more strongly convinced that these possibilities are far from being realized on account of the handling of the story in the second act. The reader feels, at the end, confused and unsatisfied: —the underlying motive of the play has not been sent home. And yet this motive, or idea, has been sufficiently perceived to prevent the play from being a sheer burlesque, like a comic opera. In the second act it seems to me that you yourself have almost thought it *was* that.

The underlying idea, a mighty good one, is expressed, or should be, in the story of Jerry Frost.

God meant Jerry to be a good egg and a postman; but having been created, in a democratic age, Free and Equal, he was persuaded that he ought to want to rise in the world and so had become a railroad clerk against his taste and capacity, and thought he ought to want to become President. He is therefore very unhappy, and so is his wife, who holds the same democratic doctrine.

Your story shows, or should, that this doctrine is sentimental bunk; and to do this is worthwhile because the doctrine is almost universal: Jerry and his wife are products of a theory of democracy which you reduce to the absurd. The idea is so good that if you hold to it and continuously develop it, your play, however successful simply as fun, will be deeply significant as well.

Moreover, the means you have selected to develop the idea are superb—the bootlegger, the super-jag his concoction induces, Jerry thereby becoming President, etc. (and dreams have a real validity nowadays on account of Freud). In fact all your machinery for expressing the idea is exactly in the tune of the time and inherently funny and satirical.

But when you come to the second act, which is the critical point in the play, and so in the expression of your idea, you seem to lose sense of your true motive. Partly, this is because you have three motives here, the main motive of Jerry's story and its meaning, and two subordinate motives—(1) of conveying through the fantastic visions and incidents which are the stuff of a dream caused by a 1923 prohibition brew, *the sense of a comic nightmare,* and (2) of satirizing the general phenomena of our national scene. You have, I think, simply got more or less lost in the maze of these three motives by a failure to follow the green line of the chief one—Jerry's actual story, or that stage of it which shows him that he *doesn't* want to be President. Satirize as much as you can, the government, the army, and everything else, and be as fantastic as you please, but keep one eye always on your chief motive. Throughout the entire wild second act there should still be a kind of *wild logic.*

Aside then from imparting in this act the sense of a dream, you are using the difficult weapon of double edged satire—you are satirizing the conception held by Jerry and his like of the High Offices of President, Secretary of the Treasury, etc., and you are at the same time satirizing those high offices themselves. You begin excellently by making all the appurtenances of the Presidency, like the house, white; and the behavior of Jerry's wife and sister-in-law are all within the scope of your purpose. The conduct of Dada as Secretary of the Treasury seems as though it ought to be a fine piece of two edged satire cutting both against the popular idea of the business of that official and against the official himself as he usually is, but the psychology of it is not made quite comprehensible; and the best instance of double satire is seen when General Pushing appears with fifer and drummer and medals— that is just the right note. Why couldn't you do the same for bankers, and senators, etc.?

Maybe I can better express what I mean by examples. The selection of so obscure a man as Jerry for President is itself the stuff of satire in view of present political methods, and much could be made of it. The coffin episode as you use it results as things do in a dream from Jerry's talk with Fish etc. and so it helps to give the sense of a dream, and that is all it does. But suppose coffins were being cornered by "The He-Americans Bloodred Preparedness League" as a preparedness measure, and that this was tied up with General Pushing's feeling that a war was needed:— that would be a hit at extravagant patriotism and militarism as well as having its present value as part of a dream. Suppose the deal over the Buzzard Isles resulted in the Impeachment of Jerry—what a chance that would give to treat the Senate as you have the general and the Army, and also to bring Jerry's affairs to a climax. You could have Jerry *convicted,* and then (as a hit at a senatorial filibuster) you could have his party place the Stutz-Mozart Ourangatang Band outside the Capitol (it would have appeared for the wedding of Fish), and every time the Justices of the Supreme Court began in chorus to pronounce the sentence, Stutz-Mozart would strike up the National Anthem in syncopated time and everyone would have to stand at attention. At present, the narrative of the second act lacks all logic; the significance of the approaching end of the world eludes me,—except as a dreamer's way of getting release from a desperate situation.

I've now used a great many words to make this single point:—each part of the second act should do three things—add to the quality of a fantastic dream, satirize Jerry and his family as representing a large class of Americans, and satirize the government or army or whatever institution is at the moment in use. And my only excuse for all this verbiage is, that so good in conception is your motive, so true your characters, so splendidly imaginative your invention, and so altogether above the mere literary the whole scheme, that no one could help but greatly desire to see it all equalled in execution. If it were a comparative trifle, like many a short story, it wouldn't much matter.

Fitzgerald was obviously intrigued by the idea of using a President's impeachment as the climax of Act II. In fact, this new development led to the highlight of the entire play: President Frost's oration in his own defense, a perfect piece of impassioned rhetoric that says absolutely nothing. It is also a virtuoso performance in mixing metaphors:

JERRY [nervously]. Gentlemen, before you take this step into your hands I want to put my best foot forward. Let us consider a few aspects. For instance, for the first aspect let us take, for example, the War of the Revolution. There was ancient Rome, for example. Let us not only live so that our children who live after us, but also that our ancestors who preceded us fought to make this country what it is!

General applause.

And now, gentlemen, a boy to-day is a man to-morrow —or, rather, in a few years. Consider the winning of the West—Daniel Boone and Kit Carson, and in our own time Buffalo Bill and—Jesse James!

Prolonged applause.

Finally, in closing, I want to tell you about a vision of mine that I seem to see. I seem to see Columbia— Columbia—ah—blindfolded—ah—covered with scales—driving the ship of state over the battle-fields of the republic into the heart of the golden West and the cotton-fields of the sunny South.

Great applause. Mr. Jones, with his customary thoughtfulness, serves a round of cocktails.

But if Fitzgerald exploited this scene to satirize political speeches he also found an opportunity to carry the satire a step further by injecting some real history into his fantasy. The subsequent declaration of impeachment by Chief

Justice Fossile, for all its absurdity, was no mere play of the author's imagination. Rather, he had turned to his history books and had lifted almost verbatim the opening speech of Congressman George Boutwell of Massachusetts at President Andrew Johnson's impeachment hearings: "In the Southern Heavens, near the Southern Cross, there is a vast space which the uneducated call a hole in the sky, where the eye of man, with the aid of the powers of the telescope, has been unable to discover nebulae, or asteroid, or comet, or planet, or star or sun. In that dreary, dark, cold region of space... the Great Author of the celestial mechanism has left the chaos which was in the beginning. If the earth was capable of the sentiments and emotions of justice and virtue... it would heave and throw... and project this enemy of two races of men into that vast region, there forever to exist in a solitude eternal as life...." Paradoxically, if we compare this quotation with Fitzgerald's version (pages 109-10) we discover that the caricatured Chief Justice is actually *less verbose* than his historical counterpart. The author must have thoroughly enjoyed this delicious bit of irony.

In January of 1923, Fitzgerald sent Perkins a list of ideas for the play. He wanted John Held, Jr., the originator of the cartoon "flapper," to design the jacket cover with "little figures—Dada, Jerry, Doris, Charlotte, Fish, Snooks and Gen Pershing [*sic*] scattered over it." The popular cartoonist followed the author's wishes and brilliantly captured the spirit of the play. This is one book that can be judged fairly by its cover, and so that original design has been kept for this present edition. Fitzgerald also requested that it "be advertised, it seems to me rather as a book of humor ... than like a play—because of course it is written to be read." This remark contained an unfortunate truth, as the eventual performance would demonstrate. For all its revisions, *The Vegetable* remained a novelist's, not a dramatist's, play, in which the lengthy stage directions often provide the most entertaining moments. Fitzgerald also suggested writing a preface and inserting "the subtitle 'or from President to postman' (note small p.)."

He never wrote the preface, but when the book went to press its title had been changed once again, to *The Vegetable,* and was accompanied by a quotation "from a current magazine" on the title page:

> *Any man who doesn't want to get on in the world, to make a million dollars, and maybe even park his toothbrush in the White House, hasn't got as much to him as a good dog has—he's nothing more or less than a vegetable.*

It has been suggested that Fitzgerald got his idea for the final title from a passage in H. L. Mencken's essay "On Being an American": "Here is a country in which it is an axiom that a businessman shall be a member of the Chamber of Commerce, an admirer of Charles M. Schwab, a reader of *The Saturday Evening Post,* a golfer—in brief, a vegetable." If so, Fitzgerald obviously reversed the meaning of Mencken's epithet with a kind of deadpan irony, which was later enriched by having Charlotte discover the quotation in her *Saturday Evening Post* (see Appendix II). But Fitzgerald's dramatic satire is never as severe as Mencken's, whatever his debt to the essayist may have been. It owed at least as much to his college days in the Triangle Club. The result is rather a mixture of satire and slapstick. One senses a basic indecisiveness beneath the banter, as though he were a composer who had forgotten his key and had begun a seemingly endless series of modulations. This was not the material for success in performance, no matter how entertaining it might be for the reader.

The book received mixed reviews, some enthusiastic in their praise. Although late in life Edmund Wilson claimed that he had never approved of the published version, that Fitzgerald had taken "too much advice" and had "ruined the whole thing," nevertheless he was perhaps the most laudatory. In his review for *Vanity Fair* Wilson wrote that Fitzgerald's play "is, in some ways, one of the best things he has done. In it he has a better idea than he usually has of what theme he wants to develop, and it does not, as his novels sometimes have, carry him into regions beyond his powers of flight. It is a fantastic and satiric comedy carried off with exhilarating humor. One has always felt that Mr. Fitzgerald ought to write dialogue for the stage and this comedy would seem to prove it. I do not know of any dialogue by an American which is lighter, more graceful or more witty. His spontaneity makes his many bad jokes go and adds a glamor to his really good ones."

Another reviewer found that "Fitzgerald's first act is Sinclair Lewis, his last act is James M. Barrie—and his middle act is nightmare." And still another called the play "a caricature of a caricature." Many saw only nonsensical riot; others, genuine satire. One critic even considered it "the most moral book in years," the moral being simply that "what the country needs is more good postmen and fewer bad Presidents." For a brief moment it even made the best-seller list.

Encouraged, Fitzgerald placed the script with Sam Harris, who scheduled it for a fall production. During the summer Fitzgerald commuted to New York from Long Island to attend rehearsals and make still more changes for the acting script (see Appendix II). The play finally opened on Monday, November 19, 1923, at Nixon's Apollo Theatre in Atlantic City. Ernest Truex played the title role—"the best postman in the world," as Fitzgerald inscribed the play to him. It was a disaster or, in the author's own wry words, a "colossal Frost." It closed almost immediately. Fitzgerald's hopes for fortune in the theater evaporated, and he was forced to turn out a spate of short stories to improve his financial situation. His *literary* "recovery" was to take another two years and a new novel, *The Great Gatsby* (1925). After his first disappointment, Fitzgerald never really regained interest in the play. Later there were to be a few revivals, mostly by amateur groups, and even some talk of selling movie rights. But except for a momentary worry in 1932 that Ryskind and Kaufman had plagiarized *The Vegetable* in *Of Thee I Sing,* he gave his play little further thought. In his opinion, the whole venture had simply been a wasted year and a half.

But was it? The constant revising, the special demands imposed by a play—a short, carefully constructed work—

coming after the sprawling *Beautiful and Damned* proved an ideal exercise for a young writer. Though the final piece was flawed, Fitzgerald had nevertheless gained valuable experience in literary craftsmanship. In an indirect way, *The Vegetable* prepared him for writing *The Great Gatsby*. And it may be more than pure coincidence that shortly after its publication *Gatsby* was adapted for the stage by Owen Davis and was a success on Broadway. Unfortunately Fitzgerald was abroad and was unable to attend its happy opening night.

Possibly *The Vegetable* was, above all, a victim of bad timing. The audience at Atlantic City in 1923 was still unaware of most of the scandals surrounding their deceased President. It was not until a year later that the lid blew off Teapot Dome. Fitzgerald's political fantasy contained far more truth than the audience was prepared to take in. But a half-century later, after one near-impeachment and with much useful hindsight, this not-so-fantastic spoof can be experienced afresh. Interestingly enough, it has already enjoyed several successful revivals abroad: in the Netherlands, France, Czechoslovakia, and England. Evidently, Fitzgerald's caricature of the American dream and its political system is more entertaining on the foreign stage. Whatever its appeal for those still on the home front, *The Vegetable* at the very least presents a new facet of Fitzgerald's life and work. As his daughter recently pointed out, "It was one of his few efforts, until much later in his life, to write about the country outside of its country clubs."

Charles Scribner III

THE VEGETABLE

THE VEGETABLE

ACT I

This is the "living" room of Jerry Frost's house. It is evening. The room (and, by implication, the house) is small and stuffy—it's an awful bother to raise these old-fashioned windows; some of them stick, and besides it's extravagant to let in much cold air, here in the middle of March. I can't say much for the furniture, either. Some of it's instalment stuff, imitation leather with the grain painted on as an after-effect, and some of it's dingily, depressingly old. That bookcase held "Ben Hur" when it was a best-seller, and it's now trying to digest "A Library of the World's Best Literature" and the "Wit and Humor of the United States in Six Volumes." That couch would be dangerous to sit upon without a map showing the location of all craters, hillocks, and thistle-patches. And three dead but shamefully unburied clocks stare eyelessly before them from their perches around the walls.

Those walls—God! The history of American photography hangs upon them. Photographs of children with

3

puffed dresses and depressing leers, taken in the Fauntleroy nineties, of babies with toothless mouths and idiotic eyes, of young men with the hair cuts of '85 and '90 and '02, and with neckties that loop, twist, snag, or flare in conformity to some esoteric, antiquated standard of middle-class dandyism. And the girls! You'd have to laugh at the girls! Imitation Gibson girls, mostly; you can trace their histories around the room, as each of them withered and staled. Here's one in the look-at-her-little-toes-aren't-they-darling period, and here she is later when she was a little bother of ten. Look! This is the way she was when she was after a husband. She might be worse. There's a certain young charm or something, but in the next picture you can see what five years of general housework have done to her. You wouldn't turn your eyes half a degree to watch her in the street. And that was taken six years ago—now she's thirty and already an old woman.

You've guessed it. That last one, allowing for the photographer's kind erasure of a few lines, is Mrs. Jerry Frost. If you listen for a minute, you'll hear her, too.

But wait. Against my will, I'll have to tell you a few sordid details about the room. There's got to be a door in plain sight that leads directly outdoors, and then there are two other doors, one to the dining-room and one

*to the second floor—you can see the beginning of the
stairs. Then there's a window somewhere that's used
in the last act. I hate to mention these things, but
they're part of the plot.*

*Now you see when the curtain went up, Jerry Frost had
left the little Victrola playing and wandered off to the
cellar or somewhere, and Mrs. Jerry (you can call
her Charlotte) hears it from where she is up-stairs.
Listen!*

"Some little bug is going to find you, so-o-ome day!"

*That's her. She hasn't got much of a voice, has she? And
she will sing one key higher than the Victrola. And
now the darn Victrola's running down and giving off
a ghastly minor discord like the death agony of a
human being.*

CHARLOTTE. [*She's up-stairs, remember.*] Jerry, wind
up the graphophone.

There's no answer.

Jer-ry!

Still no answer.

Jerry, wind up the graphophone. It isn't good for it.

Yet again no answer.

All right—[*smugly*]—if you want to ruin it, *I* don't care.

The phonograph whines, groans, gags, and dies, and almost simultaneously with its last feeble gesture a man comes into the room, saying: "What?" He receives no answer. It is Jerry Frost, in whose home we are.

Jerry Frost is thirty-five. He is a clerk for the railroad at $3,000 a year. He possesses no eyebrows, but nevertheless he constantly tries to knit them. His lips are faintly pursed at all times, as though about to emit an enormous opinion upon some matter of great importance.

On the wall there is a photograph of him at twenty-seven—just before he married. Those were the days of his high yellow pompadour. That is gone now, faded like the rest of him into a docile pattern without grace or humor.

After his mysterious and unanswered "What?" Jerry stares at the carpet, surely not in æsthetic approval, and becomes engrossed in his lack of thoughts. Suddenly he gives a twitch and tries to reach with his hand some delicious sector of his back. He can almost reach it, but not quite—poor man!—so he goes to the mantelpiece and rubs his back gently, pleasingly, against it, meanwhile keeping his glance focussed darkly upon the carpet.

He is finished. He is at physical ease again. He leans over the table—did I say there was a table?—and turns the pages of a magazine, yawning meanwhile and tentatively beginning a slow clog step with his feet. Presently this distracts him from the magazine, and he looks apathetically at his feet. Then suddenly he sits in a chair and begins to sing, unmusically, and with faint interest, a piece which is possibly his own composition. The tune varies considerably, but the words have an indisputable consistency, as they are composed wholly of the phrase: "Everybody is there, everybody is there!"

He is a motion-picture of tremendous, unconscious boredom.

Suddenly he gives out a harsh, bark-like sound and raises his hand swiftly, as though he were addressing an audience. This fails to amuse him; the arm falters, strays lower——

JERRY. Char-*lit!* Have you got the Saturday Evening Post?

There is no reply.

Char-*lit!*

Still no reply.

Char-*lit!*

CHARLOTTE [*with syrupy recrimination*]. You didn't bother to answer me, so I don't think I should bother to answer you.

JERRY [*indignant, incredulous*]. Answer you what?

CHARLOTTE. You know what I mean.

JERRY. I mos' certainly do not.

CHARLOTTE. I asked you to wind up the graphophone.

JERRY [*glancing at it indignantly*]. The phonograph?

CHARLOTTE. Yes, the graphophone!

JERRY. It's the first time I knew it. [*He is utterly disgusted. He starts to speak several times, but each time he hesitates. Disgust settles upon his face, in a heavy pall. Then he remembers his original question.*] Have you got the Saturday Evening Post?

CHARLOTTE. *Yes,* I told you!

JERRY. You did not tell me!

CHARLOTTE. I can't help it if you're deaf!

JERRY. Deaf? Who's deaf? [*After a pause.*] No more deaf than you are. [*After another pause.*] Not half as much.

CHARLOTTE. Don't talk so loud—you'll wake the people next door.

JERRY [*incredulously*]. The people next door!

CHARLOTTE. You heard me!

*Jerry is beaten, and taking it very badly. He is be-
ginning to brood when the telephone rings. He
answers it.*

JERRY. Hello! . . . [*With recognition and rising interest.*] Oh, hello. . . . Did you get the stuff. . . .
Just one gallon is all I want. . . . No, I can't use more
than one gallon. . . . [*He looks around thoughtfully.*]
Yes, I suppose so, but I'd rather have you mix it before
you bring it. . . . Well, about nine o'clock, then. [*He
rings off, gleeful now, smiling. Then sudden worry, and
the hairless eyebrows knit together. He takes a note-book
out of his pocket, lays it open before him, and picks up the
receiver.*] Midway 9191. . . . Yes. . . . Hello, is this
Mr.—Mr. S-n-o-o-k-s's residence? . . . Hello, is this
Mr. S-n-o-o-k-s's residence? . . . [*Very distinctly.*] Mr.
Snukes or Snooks. . . . Mr. S-n-, the boo—the fella
that gets *stuff*, hooch . . . h-o-o-c-h. . . . No, Snukes
or Snooks is the man I want. . . . Oh. Why, a fella
down-town gave me your husband's name and he called
me up—at least, I called him up first, and then he called
me up just now—see? . . . You see? Hello—is this
—am I talking to the wife of the—of the—of the fella
that gets *stuff* for you? The b-o-o-t-l-e-g-g-e-r? Oh,
you know, the bootlegger. [*He breathes hard after this
word. Do you suppose Central will tell on him?*] . . . Oh.
Well, you see, I wanted to tell him when he comes to-
night to come to the back door. . . . No, Hooch is

not my name. My name is Frost. 2127 Osceola Avenue. . . . Oh, he's left already? Oh, all right. Thanks. . . . Well, good-by. . . . Well, good-by . . . good-by. [*He rings off. Again his hairless brows are knit with worry.*] Char-lit!

CHARLOTTE [*abstractedly*]. Yes?

JERRY. Charlit, if you want to read a good story, read the one about the fella who gets shipwrecked on the Buzzard Islands and meets the Chinese girl, only she isn't a Chinese girl at all.

CHARLOTTE [*she's still up-stairs, remember*]. What?

JERRY. There's one story in there—are you reading the Saturday Evening Post?

CHARLOTTE. I would be if you didn't interrupt me every minute.

JERRY. I'm not. I just wanted to tell you there's one story in there about a Chinese girl who gets wrecked on the Buzzard Islands that isn't a Chinese——

CHARLOTTE. Oh, let up, for heaven's sakes! Don't *nag* me.

Clin-n-ng! That's the door-bell.

There's the door-bell.

JERRY [*with fine sarcasm*]. Oh, really? Why, I thought it was a cow-bell.

CHARLOTTE [*witheringly*]. Ha-ha!

Well, he's gone to the door. He opens it, mumbles something, closes it. Now he's back.

JERRY. It wasn't anybody.

CHARLOTTE. It must have been.

JERRY. What?

CHARLOTTE. It couldn't have rung itself.

JERRY [*in disgust*]. Oh, gosh, you think that's funny. [*After a pause.*] It was a man who wanted 2145. I told him this was 2127, so he went away.

Charlotte is now audibly descending a crickety flight of stairs, and here she is! She's thirty, and old for her age, just like I told you, shapeless, slack-cheeked, but still defiant. She would fiercely resent the statement that her attractions have declined ninety per cent since her marriage, and in the same breath she would assume that there was a responsibility and shoulder it on her husband. She talks in a pessimistic whine and, with a sort of dowdy egotism, considers herself generally in the right. Frankly, I don't like her, though she can't help being what she is.

CHARLOTTE. I thought you were going to the Republican Convention down at the Auditorium.

JERRY. Well, I am. [*But he remembers the b-o-o—.*] No, I can't.

CHARLOTTE. Well, then, for heaven's sakes don't spend the evening sitting here and nagging me. I'm nervous enough as it is.

They both sit. She produces a basket of sewing, selects a man's nightshirt and begins, apparently, to rip it to pieces. Meanwhile Jerry, who has picked up a magazine, regards her out of the corner of his eye. During the first rip he starts to speak, and again during the second rip, but each time he restrains himself with a perceptible effort.

JERRY. What are you tearing that up for?

CHARLOTTE [*sarcastically*]. Just for fun.

JERRY. Why don't you tear up one of your own?

CHARLOTTE [*exasperated*]. Oh, I know what I'm doing. For heaven's sakes, don't *n-a-a-ag* me!

JERRY [*feebly*]. Well, I just asked you. [*A long pause.*] Well, I got analyzed to-day.

CHARLOTTE. What?

JERRY. I got analyzed.

CHARLOTTE. What's that?

JERRY. I got analyzed by an expert analyzer. Everybody down at the Railroad Company got analyzed. [*Rather importantly.*] They got a chart about me that long. [*He expresses two feet with his hands.*] Say— [*He rises suddenly and goes up close to her.*] What color my eyes?

CHARLOTTE. Don't ask me. Sort of brown, I guess.

JERRY. Brown? That's what I told 'em. But they got me down for blue.

CHARLOTTE. What was it all about? Did they pay you anything for it?

JERRY. Pay me anything? Of course not. It was for my benefit. It'll do me a lot of good. I was *analyzed*, can't you understand? They found out a lot of stuff about me.

CHARLOTTE [*dropping her work in horror*]. Do you think you'll lose your job?

JERRY [*in disgust*]. A lot you know about business methods. Don't you ever read "Efficiency" or the "Systematic Weekly"? It's a sort of examination.

CHARLOTTE. Oh, I know. When they feel all the bumps on your head.

JERRY. No, not like that at all. They ask you questions, see?

CHARLOTTE. Well, you needn't be so cross about it.

He hasn't been cross.

I hope you had the spunk to tell them you thought you deserved a better position than you've got.

JERRY. They didn't ask me things like that. It was up-stairs in one of the private offices. First the character analyzer looked at me sort of hard and said "Sit down!"

CHARLOTTE. Did you sit down?

JERRY. Sure; the thing is to do what they tell you. Well, then the character analyzer asked me my name and whether I was married.

CHARLOTTE [*suspiciously*]. What did you tell her?

JERRY. Oh, it was a man. I told him yes, of course. What do you think I am?

CHARLOTTE. Well, did he ask you anything else about me?

JERRY. No. He asked me what it was my ambition to be, and I said I didn't have any ambition left, and then I said, "Do you mean when I was a kid?" And he said, "All right, what did you want to do then?" And I said "Postman," and he said, "What sort of a job would you like to get now?" and I said, "Well, what have you got to offer?"

CHARLOTTE. Did he offer you a job?

JERRY. No, he was just kidding, I guess. Well, then, he asked me if I'd ever done any studying at home to fit me for a higher position, and I said, "Sure," and he said, "What?" and I couldn't think of anything off-hand, so I told him I took music lessons. He said no, he meant about railroads, and I said they worked me so hard that when I got home at night I never want to hear about railroads again.

CHARLOTTE. Was that all?

JERRY. Oh, there were some more questions. He asked me if I'd ever been in jail.

CHARLOTTE. What did you tell him?

JERRY. I told him "no," of course.

CHARLOTTE. He probably didn't believe you.

JERRY. Well, he asked me a few more things, and then he let me go. I think I got away with it all right. At least he didn't give me any black marks on my chart —just a lot of little circles.

CHARLOTTE. Oh, you got away with it "all right." That's all you care. You got away with it. Satisfied with nothing. Why didn't you talk right up to him: "See here, I don't see why I shouldn't get more money." That's what you'd have ought to said. He'd of respected you more in the end.

JERRY [*gloomily*]. I did have ambitions once.

CHARLOTTE. Ambition to do what? To be a postman. That was a fine ambition for a fella twenty-two years old. And you'd have been one if I'd let you. The only other ambition you ever had was to marry me. And that didn't last long.

JERRY. I know it didn't. It lasted one month too long, though.

A mutual glare here—let's not look.

And I've had other ambitions since then—don't you worry.

CHARLOTTE [*scornfully*]. What?

JERRY. Oh, that's all right.

CHARLOTTE. What, though? I'd like to know what. To win five dollars playing dice in a cigar store?

JERRY. Never you mind. Don't you worry. Don't you fret. It's all right, see?

CHARLOTTE. You're afraid to tell me.

JERRY. No, I'm not. Don't you worry.

CHARLOTTE. Yes, you are.

JERRY. All right then. If you want to know, I had an ambition to be President of the United States.

CHARLOTTE [*laughing*]. Ho—*ho*—ho—*ho!*

Jerry is pretending to be interested only in sucking his teeth—but you can see that he is both sorry he made his admission and increasingly aware that his wife is being unpleasant.

CHARLOTTE. But you decided to give that up, eh?

JERRY. Sure. I gave up everything when I got married.

CHARLOTTE. Even gave up being a postman, eh? That's right. Blame it all on me! Why, if it hadn't been for me you wouldn't even be what you are—a fifty-dollar-a-week clerk.

JERRY. That's right. I'm only a fifty-dollar-a-week clerk. But you're only a thirty-dollar-a-week wife.

CHARLOTTE. Oh, I am, am I?

JERRY. I made a big mistake when I married you.

CHARLOTTE. Stop talking like that! I wish you were dead—dead and buried—cremated! Then I could have some fun.

JERRY. Where—in the poorhouse?

CHARLOTTE. That's where I'd be, I know.

Charlotte is not really very angry. She is merely smug and self-satisfied, you see, and is only mildly annoyed at this unexpected resistance to her browbeating. She knows that Jerry will always stay and slave for her. She has begun this row as a sort of vaudeville to assuage her nightly boredom.

CHARLOTTE. Why didn't you think of these things before we got married?

JERRY. I did, a couple of times, but you had me all signed up then.

The sound of uncertain steps creaking down the second floor. Into the room at a wavering gait comes Jerry's father, Horatio—"Dada."

Dada was born in 1834, and will never see eighty-eight again—in fact, his gathering blindness prevented him from seeing it very clearly in the first place. Originally he was probably Jerry's superior in initiative, but he did not prosper, and during the past twenty years his mind has been steadily failing. A Civil War pension has kept him quasi-independent, and he looks down as from a great dim height upon Jerry (whom he thinks of as an adolescent) and Charlotte (whom he rather dislikes). Never given to reading in his youth, he has lately become absorbed in the Old Testament and in all Old Testament literature, over which he burrows every day in the Public Library.

In person he is a small, shrivelled man with a great amount of hair on his face, which gives him an unmistakable resemblance to a French poodle. The fact that he is almost blind and even more nearly deaf contributes to his aloof, judicial pose, and to the prevailing impression that something grave and thoughtful and important is going on back of those faded, vacant eyes. This conception is entirely erroneous. Half the time his mind is a vacuum, in which confused clots of information and misinformation drift and stir—the rest of the time he broods upon the minute details of his daily existence. He is too old, even, for the petty spites which represent to the aged the single gesture of vitality they can make against the ever-increasing pressure of life and youth.

When he enters the room he looks neither to left nor right, but with his head shaking faintly and his

*mouth moving in a shorter vibration, makes directly
for the bookcase.*

JERRY. Hello, Dada.

Dada does not hear.

JERRY [*louder*]. Looking for the Bible, Dada?

DADA. [*He has reached the bookcase, and he turns
around stiffly.*] I'm not deaf, sir.

JERRY. [*Let's draw the old man out.*] Who do you
think will be nominated for President, Dada?

DADA [*trying to pretend he has just missed one word*].
The——

JERRY [*louder*]. Who do you think'll be nominated
for President, to-night?

DADA. I should say that Lincoln was our greatest
President. [*He turns back to the bookcase with an air of
having settled a trivial question for all time.*]

JERRY. I mean to-night. They're getting a new one.
Don't you read the papers?

DADA [*who has heard only a faint murmur*]. Hm.

CHARLOTTE. You *know* he never reads anything but
the Bible. Why do you nag him?

JERRY. He reads the encyclopædia at the Public
Library. [*With a rush of public spirit.*] If he'd just
read the newspapers he'd know what was going on and

have something to talk about.   He just sits around and
never says anything.

CHARLOTTE.   At least he doesn't gabble his head off
all day.   He's got sense enough not to do that *any*way,
haven't you, Dada?

Dada does not answer.

JERRY.   Lookit here, Charlit.   I don't call it gabbling
if I meet a man in the street and he says, "Well, I see
somebody was nominated for President," and I say,
"Yes, I see saw—see so."   Suppose I said, "Yes, Lincoln was our greatest President."   He'd say, "Why, if
that fella isn't a piece of cheese I never saw a piece of
cheese."

DADA [*turning about plaintively*].   Some one has taken
my Bible.

JERRY.   No, there it is on the second shelf, Dada.

DADA.   [*He doesn't hear.*]   I don't like people moving it around.

CHARLOTTE.   Nobody moved it.

DADA.   My old mother used to say to me, "Horatio—"
[*He brings this word out with an impressive roundness,
but as his eye, at that moment, catches sight of the Bible, he
loses track of his thought.   He pounces upon the Holy
Book and drags it out, pulling with it two or three other
books, which crash to the floor.   The sound of their fall is
very faint on his ears—and under the delusion that his*

*error is unnoticed, he slyly kicks the books under the book-
case. Jerry and Charlotte exchange a glance. With his
Bible under his arm Dada starts stealthily toward the stair-
case. He sees something bright shining on the first step,
and, not without difficulty, stoops to pick it up. His efforts
are unsuccessful.*] Hello, here's a nail that looks just
like a ten-cent piece. [*He starts up-stairs.*]

JERRY. He thought he found a ten-cent piece.

CHARLOTTE [*significantly*]. Nobody has yet in *this*
house.

> *In the ensuing silence Dada can be heard ascending
> the stairs. About half-way up there is a noise as if
> he had slipped down a notch. Then a moment of
> utter silence.*

JERRY. You all right, Dada?

No answer. Dada is heard to resume his climb.
He was just resting. [*He goes over and starts picking up
the books. Cli-n-ng! There's the front door-bell again.
It occurs to him that it's the b-o-o.*] I'll answer it.

CHARLOTTE [*who has risen*]. *I'll* answer it. It's my
own sister Doris, I *know*. You answered the last one.

JERRY. That was a mistake. It's my turn this time
by rights.

> *Answering the door-bell is evidently a pleasant diver-
> sion over which they have squabbled before.*

CHARLOTTE. I'll answer it.

JERRY. You needn't bother.

Cli-n-ng! An impatient ring that.

CHARLOTTE AND JERRY [*together*]. Now, listen here—

> *They both start for the door. Jerry turns, only trying to argue with her some more, and what does the woman do but slap his face! Then, quick as a flash, she is by him and has opened the door.*
>
> *What do you think of that? Jerry stands there with an expressionless face. In comes Charlotte's sister Doris.*
>
> *Well, now, I'll tell you about Doris. She's nineteen, I guess, and pretty. She's nice and slender and dressed in an astonishingly close burlesque of the current fashions. She's a member of that portion of the middle-class whose girls are just a little bit too proud to work and just a little bit too needy not to. In this city of perhaps a quarter of a million people she knows a few girls who know a few girls who are "social leaders," and through this connection considers herself a member of the local aristocracy. In her mind, morals, and manners she is a fairly capable imitation of the current moving-picture girl, with overtones of some of the year's débutantes whom she sees down-town. Doris knows each débutante's first name and reputation, and she follows the vari-*

*ous affairs of the season as they appear in the
society column.*

*She walks—walks, not runs—haughtily into the room,
her head inclined faintly forward, her hips motion-
less. She speaks always in a bored voice, raising
her eyebrows at the important words of each sentence.*

DORIS. Hello, people.

JERRY [*a little stiffly—he's mad.*] Why, hello, Doris.

*Doris sits down with a faint glance at her chair, as
though suspecting its chastity.*

DORIS. Well, I'm engaged again.

*She says this as though realizing that she is the one
contact this couple have with the wider and outer
world. She assumes with almost audible conde-
scension that their only objective interest is the fasci-
nating spectacle of her career. And so there is
nothing personal in her confidences; it is as though
she were reporting dispassionately an affair of
great national, or, rather, passional importance.
And, indeed, Jerry and Charlotte respond magnificently to her initial remark by saying "Honestly?"
in incredulous unison and staring at her with
almost bated breath.*

DORIS [*laconically*]. Last night.

CHARLOTTE [*reproachfully*]. Oh, Doris! [*flattering her, you see, by accusing her of being utterly incorrigible.*]

DORIS. I simply couldn't help it. I couldn't stand him any longer, and this new fella I'm engaged to now simply had to know—because he was keeping some girl waiting. I just couldn't stand it. The strain was awful.

CHARLOTTE. Why couldn't you stand it? What was the trouble?

DORIS [*coolly*]. He drank.

Charlotte, of course, shakes her head in sympathy.

He'd drink anything. Anything he could get his hands on. He used to drink all these mixtures and then come round to see me.

A close observer might notice that at this statement Jerry, thinking of his nefarious bargain with the b-o-o, perceptibly winces.

CHARLOTTE. Oh, that's too bad. He was such a clean-cut fella.

DORIS. Yes, Charlotte, he was clean-cut, but that was all. I couldn't stand it, honestly I couldn't. I never saw such a man, Charlotte. He took the platinum sardine. When they go up in your room and steal your six-dollar-an-ounce perfume, a girl's got to let a man go.

CHARLOTTE. I should say she has. What did he say when you broke it off?

DORIS. He couldn't say anything. He was too pie-eyed. I tied his ring on a string, hung it around his neck and pushed him out the door.

JERRY. Who's the new one?

DORIS. Well, to tell you the truth, I don't know much about him, but I'll tell you what I *do* know from what information I could gather from mutual friends, and so forth. He's not quite so clean-cut as the first one, but he's got lots of other good qualities. He comes from the State of Idaho, from a town named Fish.

JERRY. Fish? F-i-s-h?

DORIS. I think so. It was named after his uncle . . . a Mr. Fish.

JERRY [*wittily*]. They're a lot of Fish out there.

DORIS [*not comprehending*]. Well, these Fishes are very nice. They've been mayor a couple of times and all that sort of thing, if you know what I mean. His father's in business up there now.

JERRY. What business?

DORIS. He's in the funereal-parlor business.

JERRY [*indelicately*]. Oh, undertaker.

DORIS. [*She's sensitive to the word.*] Well, not exactly, but something like that. A funereal parlor is a sort of—oh, a sort of a *good* undertaking place, if you know what I mean. [*And now confidentially.*] As a matter of fact, that's the part of the thing I don't like. You see, we may have to live out in Fish, right over his father's place of business.

JERRY. Why, that's all right. Think how handy it'll be if——

CHARLOTTE. Keep still, Jerry!

JERRY. Is he in the same business as his father?

DORIS. No. At least not now. He was for a while, but the business wasn't very good and now he says he's through with it. His father's bought him an interest in one of the stores.

JERRY. A Fish store, eh?

The two women look at him harshly.

CHARLOTTE [*wriggling her shoulders with enjoyment*]. Tell us more about him.

DORIS. Well, he's wonderful looking. And he dresses, well, not loud, you know, but just *well*. And when anybody speaks to him he goes sort of— [*To express what Mr. Fish does when any one speaks to him, Doris turns her profile sharply to the audience, her chin up, her eyes half-closed in an expression of melancholy scorn.*]

CHARLOTTE. I know—like Rudolph Valentine.

DORIS [*witheringly—do you blame her?*]. Valentino.

JERRY. What does it mean when he does that?

DORIS. I don't know, just sort of—sort of passion.

JERRY. Passion!

DORIS. Emotion sort of. He's very emotional. That's one reason I didn't like the last fella I was engaged to. He wasn't very emotional. He was sort of an old cow most of the time. I've got to have somebody emotional. You remember that place in the Sheik where the fella says: "Must I play valet as well as lover?" That's the sort of thing I like.

CHARLOTTE [*darting a look at Jerry*]. I know *just* what you mean.

DORIS. He's not really as tall as I'd like him to be, but he's got a wonderful build and a good complexion. I can't stand anybody without a good complexion—can you? He calls me adorable egg.

JERRY. What does he mean by that?

DORIS [*airily*]. Oh, "egg" is just a name people use nowadays. It's considered sort of the thing.

JERRY [*awed*]. Egg?

CHARLOTTE. When do you expect to get married?

DORIS. You never can tell!

A pause, during which they all sigh as if pondering. Then Doris, with a tremendous effort at justice, switches the conversation away from herself.

DORIS [*patronizingly, condescendingly*]. How's everything going with you two? [*To Jerry.*] Does your father still read the Bible?

JERRY. Well, a lot of the time he just thinks.

DORIS. He hasn't had anything to do for the last twenty years but just think, has he?

JERRY [*impressed*]. Just think of the things he's probably thought out.

DORIS [*blasphemously*]. That old dumb-bell?

Charlotte and Jerry are a little shocked.

How's everything else been going around here?

JERRY. I got analyzed to-day at——

CHARLOTTE [*interrupting*]. The same as ever.

JERRY. I got anal——

CHARLOTTE [*to Jerry*]. I wish you'd be polite enough not to interrupt me.

JERRY [*pathetically*]. I thought you were through.

CHARLOTTE. Well, you've driven what I had to say right out of my head. [*To Doris.*] What do you think he said to-night? He said if he hadn't married me he'd be President of the United States.

At this Jerry drops his newspaper precipitately, walks in anger to the door, and goes out without speaking.
You see? Just a display of temper. But it doesn't worry *me*. [*She sighs—the shrew.*] I'm used to it.

Doris tactfully makes no reply. After a momentary silence she changes the subject.

DORIS. Well, I find I just made an awful mistake.

CHARLOTTE [*eagerly*]. Not keeping both those men for a while? That's what I think.

DORIS. No. I mean—do you remember those three dresses I had lengthened?

CHARLOTTE [*breathlessly*]. Yes.

DORIS [*tragically*]. I'll never be able to wear them.

CHARLOTTE. Why?

DORIS. There's a picture of Mae Murray in the new Motion Picture Magazine . . . my dear, half her calf!

CHARLOTTE. Really?

At this point the door leading to the dining-room opens and Jerry comes in. Looking neither to left nor to right, he marches to his lately vacated place, snatches up half his newspaper, and goes out without speaking. The two women bestow on him a careless glance and continue their discussion.

DORIS. It was just my luck. I wish I'd hemmed them like I thought of doing, instead of cutting them off. That's the way it always is. As soon as I get my hair bobbed, Marilyn Miller begins to let hers grow. And look at mine— [*She removes her hat.*] I can't do a thing with it. [*She replaces her hat.*] Been to the Bijou Theatre?

CHARLOTTE. No, what's there?

Again Jerry comes in, almost unbearably self-conscious now. The poor man has taken the wrong part of the paper. Silently, with a strained look, he makes the exchange under the intense supervision of four eyes, and starts back to his haven in the dining-room. Then he jumps as Doris speaks to him.

DORIS. Say!

JERRY [*morosely dignified*]. What?

DORIS [*with real interest*]. What makes you think you could be President?

JERRY [*to Charlotte*]. That's right. Make a fool of me in front of all your relations! [*In his excitement he bangs down his paper upon a chair.*]

CHARLOTTE. I haven't said one word—not one single solitary word—have I, Doris?

Jerry goes out hastily—without his paper!

Did I say one word, Doris? I'll leave it to you. Did I say one single word to bring down all that uproar on my head? To have him *swear* at me?

Jerry, crimson in the face, comes in, snatches up his forgotten paper, and rushes wildly out again.

He's been nagging at me all evening. He said I kept him from doing everything he wanted to. And you know very well, Doris, he'd have been a postman if it hadn't been for me. He said he wished I was dead.

It seems to me it was Charlotte who wished Jerry was dead!

He said he could get a better wife than me for thirty dollars a week.

DORIS [*fascinated*]. Did he really? Where did he say he could get her?

CHARLOTTE. That's the sort of man *he* is.

DORIS. He'd never be rich if you *gave* him the money. He hasn't got any *push*. I think a man's got to have *push*, don't you? I mean sort of *uh!* [*She gives a little grunt to express indomitable energy, and makes a sharp gesture with her hand*.] I saw in the paper about a fella that didn't have any legs or arms forty years old that was a millionaire.

CHARLOTTE. Maybe if Jerry didn't have any legs or arms he'd do better. How did this fella make it?

DORIS. I forget. Some scheme. He just thought of a scheme. That's the thing, you know—to think of some scheme. Some kind of cold cream or hair—say, I wish somebody'd invent some kind of henna that nobody could tell. Maybe Jerry could.

CHARLOTTE. He hasn't brains enough.

DORIS. Say, I saw a wonderful dog to-day.

CHARLOTTE. What kind of a dog?

DORIS. It was out walking with Mrs. Richard Barton Hammond on Crest Avenue. It was pink.

CHARLOTTE. Pink! I never saw a pink dog.

DORIS. Neither did I before. Gosh, it was cunning. . . . Well, I got to go. My fiancé is coming over at quarter to nine and we're going down to the theatre.

CHARLOTTE. Why don't you bring him over some time?

DORIS. All right. I'll bring him over after the movies if you'll be up.

> *They walk together to the door. Doris goes out and Charlotte has scarcely shut the door behind her when the bell rings again. Charlotte opens the door and then retreats half-way across the room, with an alarmed expression on her face. A man has come in, with a great gunny-sack slung over his shoulder. It is none other than Mr. Snooks or Snukes, the bootlegger.*
>
> *I wish I could introduce you to the original from whom I have taken Mr. Snooks. He is as villainous-looking a man as could be found in a year's search. He has a weak chin, a broken nose, a squint*

eye, and a three days' growth of beard. If you can imagine a race-track sport who has fallen in a pool of mud you can get an idea of his attire. His face and hands are incrusted with dirt. He lacks one prominent tooth, lacks it with a vulgar and somehow awful conspicuousness. His most ingratiating smile is a criminal leer, his eyes shift here and there upon the carpet, as he speaks in a villainous whine.

CHARLOTTE [*uneasily*]. What do you want?

Mr. Snooks leers and winks broadly, whereat Charlotte bumps back against the bookcase.

SNOOKS [*hoarsely*]. Tell your husband Sandy Claus is here.

CHARLOTTE [*calling nervously*]. Jerry, here's somebody wants to see you. He says he's—he's Santa Claus.

In comes Jerry. He sees the situation, but the appearance of the b-o-o evidently shocks him, and a wave of uneasiness passes over him. Nevertheless, he covers up these feelings with a magnificent nonchalance.

JERRY. Oh, yes. How de do? How are you? Glad to see you.

SNOOKS [*wiggling the bag, which gives out a loud, glassy clank*]. Hear it talking to you, eh?

Charlotte looks from one to the other of them darkly.

JERRY. It's all right, Charlit. I'll tend to it. You go up-stairs. You go up-stairs and read that—there's a story in the Saturday Evening Post about a Chinese girl on the Buzzard Islands that——

CHARLOTTE. I know. Who isn't a Chinese girl. Never mind that. I'll stay right here.

Jerry turns from her with the air of one who has done his best—but now—well, she must take the consequences.

JERRY [*to Snooks*]. Is this Mr. Snukes? Or Snooks?

SNOOKS. Snooks. Funny name, ain't it? I made it up. I got it off a can of tomatoes. I'm an Irish-Pole by rights. [*Meanwhile he has been emptying the sack of its contents and setting them on the table. First come two one-gallon jars, one full, the other empty. Then a square, unopened one-gallon can. Finally three small bottles and a medicine dropper.*]

CHARLOTTE [*in dawning horror*]. What's that? A still?

SNOOKS [*with a wink at Jerry*]. No, lady, this here's a wine-press.

JERRY. [*He's attempting to conciliate her.*] No, no, Charlit. Listen. This gentleman here is going to make me some gin—very, very cheap.

CHARLOTTE. Some gin!

JERRY. Yes, for cocktails.

CHARLOTTE. For whose cocktails?

JERRY. For you and me.

CHARLOTTE. Do you think *I'd* take one of the poison things?

JERRY [*to Snooks*]. They're not poison, are they?

SNOOKS. Poison! Say, lady, I'd be croaked off long ago if they was. I'd be up wid de angels! This ain't *wood* alcohol. This is *grain* alcohol. [*He holds up the gallon can, on which is the following label*]:

WOOD ALCOHOL!

POISON!

CHARLOTTE [*indignantly*]. Why, it says wood alcohol right on the can!

SNOOKS. Yes, but it ain't. I just use a wood-alcohol can, so in case I get caught. You're allowed to sell wood alcohol, see?

JERRY [*explaining to Charlotte*]. Just in case he gets caught—see?

CHARLOTTE. I think the whole performance is perfectly terrible.

JERRY. No, it isn't. Mr. Snooks has sold this to some of the swellest families in the city—haven't you, Mr. Snooks?

SNOOKS. Sure. You know old man Alec Martin?

JERRY [*glancing at Charlotte, who is stony-eyed*]. Sure. Everybody knows who *they* are.

SNOOKS. I sole 'em a gallon. And John B. Standish? I sole him five gallons and he said it was the best stuff he ever tasted.

JERRY [*to Charlotte*]. See—? The swellest people in town.

SNOOKS. I'd a got here sooner, only I got double crossed to-day.

JERRY. How?

SNOOKS. A fella down-town sold me out to the rev'-nue officers. I got stuck for two thousand dollars and four cases Haig and Haig.

JERRY. Gee, that's too bad!

SNOOKS. Aw, you never know who's straight in this game. They'll double cross you in a minute.

JERRY. Who sold you out?

SNOOKS. A fella. What do you suppose he got for it?

JERRY. What?

SNOOKS. Ten dollars. What do you know about a fella that'd sell a guy out for ten dollars? I just went right up to him and said: "Why, you Ga——"

JERRY [*nervously*]. Say, don't tell us!

SNOOKS. Well, I told him where he got off at, anyways. And then I plastered him one. An' the rev'nue officers jus' stood there and laughed. My brother 'n I are goin' 'round an' beat him up again tomorra.

JERRY [*righteously*]. He certainly deserved it.

A pause.

SNOOKS [*after a moment's brooding*]. Well, I'll fix this up for you now.

CHARLOTTE [*stiffly*]. How much is it?

SNOOKS. This? Sixteen a gallon.

JERRY [*eagerly*]. See, that makes two gallons of the stuff, Charlotte, and that's eight quarts, and eight quarts of the stuff makes sixteen quarts of cocktails. That's enough to last us—oh, three years anyhow. Just think how nice it'll be if anybody comes in. Just say: "Like a little cocktail?" "Sure." "All right." [*He makes a noise to express orange squeezing.*] Oranges! [*A noise to express the cracking of ice.*] Ice! [*A noise to express the sound of a shaker.*] Shaker! [*He pours the imaginary compound into three imaginary glasses. Then he drinks off one of the imaginary glasses and pats his stomach.*]

CHARLOTTE [*contemptuously*].   Well, I think you're a little crazy, if you ask me.

SNOOKS [*taking off his hat and coat*].   You got a big bowl?

CHARLOTTE.   No.   Why didn't you bring your own bowl?

JERRY [*uncertainly*].   There's a nice big bowl in the kitchen.

CHARLOTTE.   All right.   Go on and spoil all the kitchen things.

JERRY.   I'll wash it afterward.

CHARLOTTE.   Wash it?   [*She laughs contemptuously, implying that washing will do it no good then.   Jerry, nevertheless, goes for the bowl.   He feels pretty guilty by this time, but he's going through with it now, even though he may never hear the last of it.*]

SNOOKS [*hollering after him*].   Get a corkscrew, too. [*He holds up the tin can to Charlotte.*]   Grain alcohol. [*Charlotte's lips curl in answer.   He holds up a small bottle.*]   Spirits of Jupiter.   One drop of this will smell up a whole house for a week.   [*He holds up a second bottle.*]   Oila Aniseed.   Give it a flavor.   Take the arsenic out.   [*He holds up a third bottle.*]   Oila Coeander.

CHARLOTTE [*sardonically*].   Wouldn't you like me to look in the medicine-chest and see if there's something

there you could use? Maybe you need some iodine.
Or some of Dada's ankle-strengthener.

Jerry comes in, laden.

JERRY. Here's the bowl and the corkscrew.

CHARLOTTE. You forgot the salt and pepper.

*Amid great pounding the bootlegger breaks the cork-
screw on the tin can. His exertions send him into
a fit of coughing.*

You'll have to stop coughing. You'll wake the people
next door.

SNOOKS. You got a hairpin, lady?

CHARLOTTE. No.

SNOOKS. Or a scissors?

CHARLOTTE. No.

SNOOKS. Say, what kind of a house is this? [*He
finally manages to open the can.*]

SNOOKS. [*With some pride.*] Grain alcohol. Costs
me $6.00 a gallon. [*To Charlotte.*] Smell it.

She retreats from it hastily.

CHARLOTTE. I can smell *something* horrible.

SNOOKS. That's the spirits of Jupiter. I haven't
opened it yet. It rots a cork in ten days. [*He fills the
bowl with water from one jar.*]

JERRY [*anxiously*]. Hadn't you better measure it?

SNOOKS.   I got my eye trained.

CHARLOTTE.   What's that—arsenic?

SNOOKS.   Distilled water, lady.   If you use regular water it gets cloudy.   You want it clear.   [*He pours in alcohol from the can.*]   Got a spoon? . . .   Well, never mind.   [*He rolls up his sleeve and undoubtedly intends to plunge his whole arm into the mixture.*]

JERRY [*hastily*].   Here!   Wait a minute.   No use— no use getting your hand wet.   I'll get you a spoon. [*He goes after it.*]

CHARLOTTE [*sarcastically*].   Get one of the best silver ones.

SNOOKS.   Naw.   Any kind'll do.

Jerry returns with one of the best silver spoons, which he hands to Mr. Snooks.

CHARLOTTE.   I might have known you would—you fool!

Mr. Snooks stirs the mixture—the spoon turns rust- colored—Charlotte gives a little cry.

SNOOKS.   It won't hurt it, lady.   Just leave it out in the sun for an hour.   Now the spirits of Jupiter.   [*He fills the medicine dropper from a small bottle and lets a slow, interminable procession of drops fall into the bowl. Jerry watches intently and with gathering anxiety. At about the fourteenth drop he starts every time one falls. Finally Mr. Snooks ceases.*]

JERRY.   How many did you count?

SNOOKS.   Sixteen.

JERRY.   I counted eighteen.

SNOOKS.   Well, a drop or so won't make no difference.   Now you got a funnel?

JERRY.   I'll get one.   [*He goes for it.*]

SNOOKS.   Good stuff, lady.   This is as good as what you used to buy for the real thing.

Charlotte does not deign to answer.

You needn't worry about that spoon.   If that spoon had a been the real thing it w'na done like that.   You can try out all your stuff that way.   A lot of stuff is sold for silver nowadays that ain't at all.

Jerry returns with the funnel, and Mr. Snooks pours the contents of the bowl into the two glass jars.

SNOOKS [*holding up one jar admiringly*].   The real thing.

CHARLOTTE.   It's cloudy.

SNOOKS [*reproachfully*].   Cloudy?   You call that cloudy?   That isn't cloudy.   Why, it's just as clear——

He holds it up and pretends to look through it.   This is unquestionably a mere gesture, for the mixture is heavily opaque and not to be pierced by the human eye.

CHARLOTTE [*disregarding him and turning scornfully to Jerry*]. I wouldn't drink it if it was the last liquor in the world.

SNOOKS. Lady, if this was the last liquor in the world it wouldn't be for sale.

JERRY [*doubtfully*]. It does look a little—cloudy.

SNOOKS. No-o-o—! Why you can see right through it. [*He fills a glass and drinks it off.*] Why, it just needs to be filtered. That's just nervous matter.

CHARLOTTE AND JERRY [*together*]. Nervous matter?

JERRY. When did we put that in?

SNOOKS. We didn't put it in. It's just a deposit. Sure, that's just nervous matter. Any chemis' will tell you.

CHARLOTTE [*sardonically*]. Ha-ha! "Nervous matter." There's no such thing.

SNOOKS. Sure! That's just nervous matter. [*He fills the glass and hands it to her.*] Try it!

CHARLOTTE. Ugh!

As he comes near she leans away from him in horror. Snooks offers the glass to Jerry.

If you drink any of that stuff they'll have to analyze you all over again.

But Jerry drinks it.

CHARLOTTE. I can't stand this. When your—when *he's* gone I'll thank you to open the windows. [*She goes out and up-stairs.*]

SNOOKS [*with a cynical laugh*]. Your old lady's a little sore on you, eh?

JERRY [*bravely*]. No. She doesn't care what I do.

SNOOKS. You ought to give her a bat in the eye now and then. That'd fix her.

JERRY [*shocked*]. Oh, no; you oughtn't to talk that way.

SNOOKS. Well, if you like 'em to step around. . . . Sixteen bucks, please.

Jerry searches his pockets.

JERRY [*counting*].—thirteen—fourteen—let's see. I can borrow the ice-man's money if I can find where— Just wait a minute, Mr. Snooks.

> *He goes out to the pantry. Almost immediately there are steps upon the stairs, and in a moment Dada, resplendent in a flowing white nightshirt, trembles into Mr. Snooks's vision. For a moment Mr. Snooks is startled.*

DADA [*blinking*]. I thought I smelled something burning.

SNOOKS. I ain't smelled nothin', pop.

DADA. How do you do, sir. You'll excuse my costume. I was awake and it occurred to me that the house was on fire. I am Mr. Frost's father.

SNOOKS. I'm his bootlegger.

DADA. The——?

SNOOKS. His bootlegger.

DADA [*enthusiastically*]. You're my son's employer?

They shake hands.

DADA. Excuse my costume. I was awake, and I thought I smelled something burning.

SNOOKS [*decisively*]. You're kiddin' yourself.

DADA. Perhaps I was wrong. My sense of smell is not as exact as it was. My son Jerry is a fine boy. He's my only son by my second wife, Mr. —? The——? [*He is evidently under the impression that Snooks has supplied the name and that he has missed it.*] I'm glad to meet his employer. I always say I'm a descendant of Jack Frost. We used to have a joke when I was young. We used to say that the first Frosts came to this state in the beginning of winter. Ha-ha-ha! [*He is convinced that he is giving Jerry a boost with his employer.*]

SNOOKS [*bored*]. Ain't it past your bedtime, pop?

DADA. Do you see? "Frosts" and "frosts." We used to laugh at that joke a great deal.

SNOOKS. Anybody would.

DADA. "Frosts," you see. We're not rich, but I always say that it's easier for a camel to get through a needle's eye than for a rich man to get to heaven.

SNOOKS. That's the way I always felt.

DADA. Well, I think I'll turn in. My sense of smell deceived me. No harm done. [*He laughs.*] Good night, Mr. ——?

SNOOKS [*humorously*]. Good night, pop. Sleep tight. Don't let the bedbugs bite.

DADA [*starting away*]. I hope you'll excuse my costume. [*He goes up-stairs. Jerry returns from the pantry just in time to hear his voice.*]

JERRY. Who was that? Dada?

SNOOKS. He thought he was on fire.

JERRY [*unaware of the nightshirt*]. That's my father. He's a great authority on—oh, on the Bible and a whole lot of other things. He's been doing nothing for twenty years but thinking out a lot of things—here's the money. [*Jerry gives him sixteen bucks.*]

SNOOKS. Thanks. Well, I guess you're all fixed. Drink a couple of these and then you'll know what to say to your wife when she gets fresh.

CHARLOTTE [*from up-stairs*]. Shut the door! I can smell that way up here!

Jerry hastily shuts the door leading up-stairs.

SNOOKS. Like any whiskey?

JERRY. I don't believe so.

SNOOKS. Or some cream de menthy?

JERRY. No, I don't believe so.

SNOOKS. How about some French vermuth?

JERRY. I don't think I'll take anything else now.

SNOOKS. Just try a drink of this.

JERRY. I did.

SNOOKS. Try another.

Jerry tries another.

JERRY. Not bad. Strong.

SNOOKS. Sure it's strong. Knock you over. Hard to get now. They gyp you every time. The country's goin' to the dogs. Most of these bootleggers, you can't trust 'em two feet away. It's awful. They don't seem to have no conscience.

JERRY [*warming*]. Have you ever been analyzed, Mr. Snooks?

SNOOKS. Me? No, I never been arrested by the regular police.

JERRY. I mean when they ask you questions.

SNOOKS. Sure, I know. Thumb-prints—all that stuff.

Jerry takes another drink.

JERRY. You ought to want to rise in the world.

SNOOK. How do you know I oughta.

JERRY. Why—why, everybody ought to. It says so.

SNOOKS. What says so.

JERRY [*with a burst of inspiration*]. The Bible. It's one of the commandments.

SNOOKS. I never could get through that book.

JERRY. Won't you sit down?

SNOOKS. No, I got to hustle along in a minute.

JERRY. Say, do you mind if I ask you a personal question?

SNOOKS. Not at all. Shoot!

JERRY. Did you ever—did you ever have any ambition to be President?

SNOOKS. Sure. Once.

JERRY [*ponderously*]. You did, eh?

SNOOKS. Once. I guess bootleggin's just as good, though. More money in it.

JERRY [*weightily*]. Yes, that's true.

SNOOKS. Well, I got to hustle along now. I got to take my old woman to church.

JERRY. Oh. Yes.

SNOOKS. Well, so long. You got my address in case you go dry.

They both smile genially at this pleasantry.

JERRY [*opening the door*].   All right.   I'll remember.

*Snooks goes out.   Jerry hesitates—then he opens the
door to the up-stairs.*

JERRY.   Oh, Char-lit!

CHARLOTTE [*crossly*].   Please keep that door shut.
That smell comes right up here.   It'll start my hay-
fever.

JERRY [*genially*].   Well, I just wanted to ask you if
you'll take one little cocktail with me.

CHARLOTTE.   *No!*   How many times do I have to
tell you?

JERRY [*crestfallen*].   Well, you don't need to be so disagreeable about it.

*He receives no answer.   He would like to talk some
more, but he shuts the door and returns to the table.
Picking up one of the jars, he regards its opaque-
ness with a quizzical eye.   But it is his and quite
evidently it seems to him good.   He looks curiously
at the three little bottles, smells one of them curiously and hastily replaces the cork.   He hesitates.   Then he repairs to the dining-room, singing:
"Everybody is there!"—and returns immediately
with an orange, a knife, and another glass.   He
cuts the orange, squeezes half of it into a glass,
wipes his hands on the fringe of the tablecloth, and*

*adds some of his liquor. He drinks it slowly—he
waits. He prepares another potation with the other
half of the orange.*

*No! He does not choke, make horrible faces, nor feel
his throat as it goes down. Nor does he stagger.
His elation is evinced only by the vague confusion
with which he mislays knife, oranges, and glasses.*

*Impelled by the gregarious instinct of mankind, he
again repairs to the door that leads up-stairs, and
opens it.*

JERRY [*calling*]. Say, Char-*lit!* The convention must
be over. I wonder who was nominated.

CHARLOTTE. I asked you to shut that door.

*But the impulse to express himself, to fuse his new
elation into the common good, is irresistible. He
goes to the telephone and picks up the receiver.*

JERRY. Hello. . . . Hello, hello. Say! I wonder'f
you could tell me who was nominated for President. . . .
All right, give me Information. . . . Information, I
wonder if you could tell me who was nominated for
President. . . . Why not? . . . Well, that's informa-
tion, isn't it? . . . It doesn't matter what *kind* of in-
formation it is. It's information, isn't it? Isn't it?
It's information, isn't it? . . . Say, what's your hurry?
[*He bobs the receiver up and down.*] Hello, give me Long
Distance again. . . . Hello, is this Information? . . .

This is *mis*information, eh? Ha-ha! Did you hear that? *Mis*information. . . . I asked for Information. . . . Well, you'll do, Long Distance. . . . Long Distance—how far away are you? A long distance! Ha-ha! . . . Hello . . . Hello!

She has evidently rung off. Jerry does likewise.

JERRY [*sarcastically*]. Wonderful telephone service! [*He goes quickly back to the 'phone and picks up the receiver.*] Rottenest telephone service I ever saw! [*He slams up and returns to his drink.*]

> *There is a call outside, "Yoo-hoo!" and immediately afterward Doris opens the front door and comes in, followed by Joseph Fish, a red-headed, insipid young man of about twenty-four. Fish is dressed in a ready-made suit with a high belt at the back, and his pockets slant at a rakish angle. He is the product of a small-town high-school and a one-year business course at a state university.*
>
> *Doris has him firmly by the arm. She leads him up to Jerry, who sets down his glass and blinks at them.*

DORIS. Gosh! This room smells like a brewery. [*She notices the jars and the other débris of Jerry's domestic orgy.*] What on earth have you been doing? Brewing whiskey?

JERRY [*attempting a dignified nonchalance*]. Making cocktails.

DORIS [*with a long whistle*]. What does Charlotte say?

JERRY [*with dignity*]. Charlit is up-stairs.

DORIS. Well, I want you to meet my fiancé, Mr. Fish. Mr. Fish, this is my brother-in-law, Mr. Frost.

JERRY. Pleased to meet you, Mr. Fish.

FISH. How de do. [*He laughs politely.*]

JERRY [*horribly*]. Is this the undertaker?

DORIS [*tartly*]. You must be tight.

JERRY [*to Fish*]. Have a little drink?

DORIS. He doesn't use it.

FISH. Thanks. I don't use it. [*Again he laughs politely.*]

JERRY [*with a very roguish expression*]. Do you know Ida?

FISH. Ida who?

JERRY. Idaho. [*He laughs uproariously at his own wit.*] That's a joke I heard to-day. I thought I'd tell it to you because you're from Idaho.

FISH [*resentfully*]. Gosh, that's a rotten joke.

JERRY [*high-hatting him*]. Well, Idaho's a rotten state. I wouldn't come from that State.

DORIS [*icily*]. Maybe they'd feel the same way about

you. I'm going up and see Charlotte. I wish you'd
entertain Mr. Fish politely for a minute.

> *Doris goes up-stairs. The two men sit down. Fish
> is somewhat embarrassed.*

JERRY [*with a wink*]. Now she's gone, better have a
little drink.

FISH. No, thanks. I don't use it any more. I used
to use it a good deal out in Idaho, and then I quit.

> *A faint, almost imperceptible noise, as of a crowd far
> away, begins outside. Neither of the men seems to
> notice it, however.*

JERRY. Get good liquor up there?

FISH. Well, around the shop we used to drink embalming fluid, but it got so it didn't agree with me.

JERRY [*focussing his eyes upon Fish, with some difficulty*]. I shouldn't think it would.

FISH. It's all right for some fellas, but it doesn't
agree with me at all.

JERRY [*suddenly*]. How old are you?

FISH. Me? Twenty-five.

JERRY. Did you ever—did you ever have any ambition to be President?

FISH. President?

JERRY. Yes.

FISH. Of a company?

JERRY. No. Of the United States.

FISH [*scornfully*]. No-o-o-o!

JERRY [*almost pleadingly*]. Never did, eh?

FISH. Never.

JERRY. Tha's funny. Did you ever want to be a postman?

FISH [*scornfully*]. No-o-o-o! . . . The thing to be is to be a senator.

JERRY. Is that so?

FISH. Sure. I'm goin' to be one. Say! There's where you get the *real* graft.

Jerry's eyes close sleepily and then start open.

JERRY [*attentively*]. Do you hear a noise?

FISH [*after listening for a moment*]. I don't hear a sound.

JERRY [*puzzled*]. That's funny. I hear a noise.

FISH [*scornfully*]. I guess you're seeing things.

Another pause.

JERRY. And you say you never wanted to be President?

FISH. Na-ah!

The noise outside has now increased, come nearer, swollen to the dimensions of a roar. Presently it is almost under the windows. Fish apparently does not hear it, but Jerry knits his hairless brows and rises to his feet. He goes to the window and throws it open. A mighty cheer goes up and there is the beating of a bass drum.

JERRY. Good gosh!

Cli-in-ng! Cli-in-ng! Cli-in-ng! The door-bell! Then the door swings open, and a dozen men rush into the room. In the lead is Mr. Jones, a politician.

MR. JONES [*approaching Jerry*]. Is this Mr. Jeremiah Frost?

JERRY [*with signs of fright*]. Yes.

MR. JONES. I'm Mr. Jones, the well-known politician. I am delegated to inform you that on the first ballot you were unanimously given the Republican nomination for President.

Wild cheers from inside and out, and renewed beating of the bass drum. Jerry shakes Mr. Jones's hand, but Fish, sitting in silence, takes no heed of the proceeding—apparently does not see or hear what is going on.

JERRY [*to Mr. Jones*]. My golly! I thought you were a revenue officer.

Amid a still louder burst of cheering Jerry is elevated to the shoulders of the crowd, and borne enthusiastically out the door as

THE CURTAIN FALLS

ACT II

*Any one who felt that the First Act was perhaps a little
vulgar, will be glad to learn that we're now on the lawn
of the White House. Indeed, a corner of the Executive Mansion projects magnificently into sight, and
steps lead up to the imposing swinging doors of a
"Family Entrance." From the window of the President's office a flag flutters, and the awning displays this
legend:*

THE WHITE HOUSE

JERRY FROST, PRES.

*And if you look hard enough at the office window you can
see the President himself sitting at his desk inside.*

*The lawn, bounded by a white brick wall, is no less attrac-
tive. Not only are there white vines and flowers, a
beautiful white tree, and a white table and chairs, but,
also, a large sign over the gate, which bears the President's name pricked out in electric bulbs.*

*Two white kittens are strolling along the wall, enjoying the
ten-o'clock sunshine. A blond parrot swings in a
cage over the table, and one of the chairs is at present*

56

*occupied by a white fox-terrier puppy about the size
of your hand.*

*That's right. "Isn't it darling!" We'll let you watch it
for a moment before we move into the Whirl of Public
Affairs.*

*Look! Here comes somebody out. It's Mr. Jones, the
well-known politician, now secretary to President
Frost. He has a white broom in his hands, and, after
delighting the puppy with an absolutely white bone, he
begins to sweep off the White House steps. At this
point the gate swings open and Charlotte Frost comes
in. As befits the First Lady of the Land, she is elab-
orately dressed—in the height of many fashions. She's
evidently been shopping—her arms are full of pack-
ages—but she has nevertheless seen fit to array herself
in a gorgeous evening dress, with an interminable train.
From her wide picture hat a plume dangles almost to
the ground.*

Mr. Jones politely relieves her of her bundles.

CHARLOTTE [*abruptly*]. Good morning, Mr. Jones.
Has everything gone to pieces?

Mr. Jones looks her over in some surprise.

JONES [*apologetically*]. Well, perhaps the petti-
coat——

CHARLOTTE [*a little stiffly*].   I didn't mention myself, I don't think, Mr. Jones.   I meant all my husband's public affairs.

JONES.   He's been in his office all morning, Mrs. Frost.   There are a lot of people waiting to see him.

CHARLOTTE.   [*She's relieved.*]   I heard them calling an extra, and I thought maybe everything had gone to pieces.

JONES.   No, Mrs. Frost, the President hasn't made any bad mistake for some time now.   Of course, a lot of people objected when he appointed his father Secretary of the Treasury; his father's being so old——

CHARLOTTE.   Well, I've had to stand for his family all my life—so I guess the country can.   [*Confidentially.*]

JONES [*a little embarrassed*].   I see you've been shopping.

CHARLOTTE.   I've been buying some things for my sister's wedding reception this afternoon.

*The window of President Frost's office opens abruptly.
A white cigar emerges—followed by Jerry's hairless
eyebrows—passionately knit.*

JERRY.   All right.   Go on and yell—and then when I make some awful mistake and the country goes to pieces, blame it on me!

CHARLOTTE [*very patiently*]. Nagging me again. Picking on me. Pick—pick—pick! All day!

JERRY. Gosh, you can be disagreeable, Charlit!

CHARLOTTE. Pick—pick—pick!

JERRY [*confused*]. Pick?

CHARLOTTE [*sharply*]. Pick!

Jerry jams down his window.

Meanwhile from the window above has emerged a hand holding a mirror. The hand is presently followed by a head with the hair slicked back damply. Doris, sister-in-law to the President, is seeking more light for her afternoon toilet.

DORIS [*disapprovingly*]. I can hear you two washing your clothes in public all over the lawn.

CHARLOTTE. He keeps nagging at me.

Doris begins to apply a white lotion to her face. She daubs it at a freckle on her nose, and gazes passionately at the resultant white splotch.

DORIS [*abstractedly*]. I should think you'd get so you could stand him in public, anyways.

CHARLOTTE. He makes me madder in public than anywhere else.

She gathers her bundles and goes angrily into the White House. Doris glances down at Mr. Jones, and, deciding hastily that she is too publicly placid, withdraws her person from sight.

Jones picks up his broom and is about to go inside when a uniformed chauffeur opens the gate and announces:

"The Honorable Joseph Fish, Senator from Idaho."

And now here's Joseph Fish, in an enormous frock-coat and a tall silk hat, radiating an air of appalling prosperity.

FISH. Good morning, Mr. Jones. Is my fiancée around?

JONES. I believe she's in her boudoir, Senator Fish. How is everything down at the capital?

FISH [*gloomily*]. Awful! I'm in a terrible position, Mr. Jones—and this was to have been my wedding reception day. Listen to this. [*He takes a telegram from his pocket.*] "Senator Joseph Fish, Washington, D. C. Present the State of Idaho's compliments to President Frost and tell him that the people of Idaho demand his immediate resignation."

JONES. This is terrible!

FISH. It's because he made his father Secretary of the Treasury.

JONES. This will be depressing news to the President.

FISH. But think of *me!* This was to have been my

wedding reception day.   What will Doris say when she
hears about this.   I've got to ask her own brother-in-law
to—to move out of his home ?

JONES.   Have a cocktail.

*He takes a shaker and glasses from behind a porch
pillar and pours out two drinks.*

JONES.   I saw this coming.   But I'll tell you now,
Senator Fish, the President won't resign.

FISH.   Then it'll be my duty to have him impeached.

JONES.   Shall I call the President now ?

FISH.   Let's wait until eleven o'clock.   Give me one
more hour of happiness.   [*He raises his eyes pathetically
to the upper window.*]   Doris—oh Doris !

*Doris, now fully dressed and under the influence of
cosmetics, comes out onto the lawn.   Mr. Jones,
picking up the broom and the puppy, goes into the
White House.*

FISH [*jealously*].   Where were you all day yesterday ?

DORIS [*languidly*].   An old beau of mine came to see
me and kept hanging around.

FISH [*in wild alarm*].   Good God !   What'd he say?

DORIS.   He said I was stuck up because my brother-
in-law was President, and I said: "Well, what if I am ?
I'd hate to say what your brother-in-law is."

FISH [*fascinated*]. What is he?

DORIS. He owns a garbage disposal service.

FISH [*even more fascinated*]. Is that right? Can you notice it on his brother-in-law?

DORIS. Something awful. I wouldn't of let him come in the house. Imagine if somebody came in to see you and said: "Sniff. Sniff. Who's been sitting on these chairs?" And you said: "Oh, just my brother-in-law, the garbage disposal man."

FISH. Doris—Doris, an awful thing has occurred——

DORIS [*looking out the gate*]. Here comes Dada. Say, he must be going on to between eighty and ninety years old, if not older.

FISH [*gloomily*]. Why did your brother-in-law have to go and make him Secretary of the Treasury? He might as well have gone to an old men's home and said: "See here, I want to get eight old dumb-bells for my cabinet."

DORIS. Oh, Jerry does everything all wrong. You see, he thought his father had read a lot of books—the Bible and the Encyclopædia and the Dictionary and all.

In totters Dada. Prosperity has spruced him up, but not to any alarming extent. The hair on his face is not under cultivation. His small, watery eyes gleam dully in their ragged ovals. His mouth laps faintly at all times, like a lake with tides mildly agitated by the moon.

FISH. Good morning, Mr. Frost.

DADA [*dimly*]. Hm.

He is under the impression that he has made an adequate response.

DORIS [*tolerantly*]. Dada, kindly meet my fiancé— Senator Fish from Idaho.

DADA [*expansively*]. Young man, how do you do? I feel very well. You wouldn't think I was eighty-eight years old, would you?

FISH [*politely*]. I should say not.

DORIS. You'd think he was two hundred.

DADA [*who missed this*]. Yeah. [*A long pause.*] We used to have a joke when I was young—we used to say the first Frosts came to this country in the beginning of winter.

DORIS. Funny as a crutch.

DADA [*to Fish*]. Do you ever read the Scriptures?

FISH. Sometimes.

DADA. I'm the Secretary of the Treasury, you know. My son made me the Secretary of the Treasury. He's the President. He was my only boy by my second wife.

DORIS. The old dumb-bell!

DADA. I was born in 1834, under the presidency of Andrew Jackson. I was twenty-seven years old when the war broke out.

DORIS [*sarcastically*]. Do you mean the Revolutionary War?

DADA [*witheringly*]. The Revolutionary War was in 1776.

DORIS. Tell me something I don't know.

DADA. When you grow older you'll find there are a lot of things you don't know. [*To Fish.*] Do you know my son Jerry?

DORIS [*utterly disgusted*]. Oh, gosh!

FISH. I met your son before he was elected President and I've seen him a lot of times since then, on account of being Senator from Idaho and all, and on account of Doris. You see, we're going to have our wedding reception this afternoon——

> *In the middle of this speech Dada's mind has begun to wander. He utters a vague "Hm!" and moves off, paying no further attention, and passing through the swinging doors into the White House.*

FISH [*impressed in spite of himself by Dada's great age*]. He's probably had a lot of experience, that old bird. He was alive before you were born.

DORIS. So were a lot of other old nuts. Come on—
let's go hire the music for our wedding reception.

FISH [*remembering something with a start*]. Doris—
Doris, would you have a wedding reception with me if
you knew—if you knew the disagreeable duty——

DORIS. Knew what?

FISH. Nothing. I'm going to be happy, anyways
[*he looks at his watch*]—for almost an hour.

They go out through the garden gate.

*And now President Jerry Frost himself is seen to
leave his window and in a minute he emerges from
the Executive Mansion. He wears a loose-fitting
white flannel frock coat, and a tall white stovepipe
hat. His heavy gold watch-chain would anchor a
small yacht, and he carries a white stick, ringed with
a gold band.*

*After rubbing his back sensuously against a porch pil-
lar, he walks with caution across the lawn and his
hand is on the gate-latch when he is hailed from the
porch by Mr. Jones.*

JONES. Mr. President, where are you going?

JERRY [*uneasily*]. I thought I'd go down and get a
cigar.

JONES [*cynically*]. It doesn't look well for you to play
dice for cigars, sir.

Jerry sits down wearily and puts his hat on the table.

JONES. I'm sorry to say there's trouble in the air, Mr. President. It's what we might refer to as the Idaho matter.

JERRY. The Idaho matter?

JONES. Senator Fish has received orders from Idaho to demand your resignation at eleven o'clock this morning.

JERRY. I never liked that bunch of people they got out there in Idaho.

JONES. Well, I just thought I'd tell you—so you could think about it.

JERRY [*hopefully*]. Maybe I'll get some idea how to fix it up. I'm a very resourceful man. I always think of something.

JONES. Mr. President, would you—would you mind telling me how you got your start?

JERRY [*carelessly*]. Oh, I got analyzed one day, and they just found I was sort of a good man and would just be wasting my time as a railroad clerk.

JONES. So you forged ahead?

JERRY. Sure. I just made up my mind to be President, and then I went ahead and did it. I've always been a very ambitious sort of—sort of domineerer.

Jones sighs and takes several letters from his pocket.

JONES. The morning mail.

JERRY [*looking at the first letter*]. This one's an ad, I'll bet. [*He opens it.*] "Expert mechanics, chauffeurs, plumbers earn big money. We fit you in twelve lessons." [*He looks up.*] I wonder if there's anything personal in that. If there is it's a low sort of joke.

JONES [*soothingly*]. Oh, I don't think there is.

JERRY [*offended*]. Anybody that'd play a joke like that on a person that has all the responsibility of being President, and then to have somebody play a low, mean joke on him like that!

JONES. I'll write them a disagreeable letter.

JERRY. All right. But make it sort of careless, as if it didn't matter to me.

JONES. I can begin the letter "Damn Sirs" instead of "Dear Sirs."

JERRY. Sure, that's the idea. And put something like that in the ending, too.

JONES. "Yours insincerely," or something like that. . . . Now there's a few people waiting in here to see you, sir. [*He takes out a list.*] First, there's somebody that's been ordered to be hung.

JERRY. What about him?

JONES. I think he wants to arrange it some way so he won't be hung. Then there's a man that's got a scheme for changing everybody in the United States green.

JERRY [*puzzled*]. Green?

JONES. That's what he says.

JERRY. Why green?

JONES. He didn't say. I told him not to wait. And there's the Ambassador from Abyssinia. He says that one of our sailors on leave in Abyssinia threw the king's cousin down a flight of thirty-nine steps.

JERRY [*after a pause*]. What do you think I ought to do about that?

JONES. Well, I think you ought to—well, send flowers or something, to sort of recognize that the thing had happened.

JERRY [*somewhat awed*]. Is the king's cousin sore?

JONES. Well, naturally he——

JERRY. I don't mean sore that way. I mean did he —did he take it hard? Did he think there was any ill feeling from the United States Government in the sailor's—action?

JONES. Why, I suppose you might say yes.

JERRY. Well, you tell him that the sailor had no instructions to do any such thing. Demand the sailor's resignation.

JONES. And Major-General Pushing has been wait-

ing to see you for some time.   Shall I tell him to come
out here?

JERRY.   All right.

*Jones goes into the White House and returns, an-
nouncing: "Major-General Pushing, U. S. A."*

*Out marches General Pushing.   He is accompanied
at three paces by a fifer and drummer, who play a
spirited march.   When the General reaches the
President's table the trio halt, the fife and drum
cease playing, and the General salutes.*

*The General is a small fat man with a fierce gray
mustache.   His chest and back are fairly obliter-
ated with medals, and he is wearing one of those
great shakos peculiar to drum-majors.*

JERRY.   Good morning, General Pushing.   Did they
keep you waiting?

GENERAL PUSHING [*fiercely*].   That's all right.   We've
been marking time—it's good for some of the muscles.

JERRY.   How's the army?

GENERAL PUSHING.   Very well, Mr. President.   Several of the privates have complained of headaches.   [*He
clears his throat portentously.*]   I've called on you to say
I'm afraid we've got to have war.   I held a conference
last night with two others of our best generals.   We dis-
cussed the matter thoroughly, and then we took a vote.
Three to nothing in favor of war.

JERRY [*alarmed*]. Look at here, General Pushing, I've got a lot of things on my hands now, and the last thing I want to have is a war.

GENERAL PUSHING. I knew things weren't going very well with you, Mr. President. In fact, I've always thought that what this country needs is a military man at the head of it. The people are restless and excited. The best thing to keep their minds occupied is a good war. It will leave the country weak and shaken—but docile, Mr. President, docile. Besides—we voted on it, and there you are.

JERRY. Who is it against?

GENERAL PUSHING. That we have not decided. We're going to take up the details to-night. It depends on—just how much money there is in the Treasury. Would you mind calling up your—*father*—[*the General gives this word an ironic accentuation*]—and finding out?

Jerry takes up the white telephone from the table. Jones meanwhile has produced the shaker and glasses. He pours a cocktail for every one—even for the fifer and drummer.

JERRY [*at the 'phone*]. Connect me with the Treasury Department, please. . . . Is this the Treasury? . . . This is President Frost. . . . Oh, I'm very well, thanks. No, it's better. Much better. The dentist says he doesn't think I'll have to have it out now. . . . Say, what I called you up about is to find how much money there is in the Treasury. . . . Oh, I see. . . . Oh, I see. Thanks. [*He hangs up the receiver.*]

JERRY [*worried*]. General Pushing, things seem to be a little confused over at the Treasury. Dada—the Secretary of the Treasury isn't there right now—and they say nobody else knows much about it.

GENERAL PUSHING [*disapprovingly*]. Hm! I could put you on a nice war pretty cheap. I could manage a battle or so for almost nothing. [*With rising impatience.*] But a good President ought to be able to tell just how much we could afford.

JERRY [*chastened*]. I'll find out from Dada.

GENERAL PUSHING [*meaningly*]. Being President is a sacred trust, you know, Mr. Frost.

JERRY. Well, I know it's a sacred trust, don't I?

GENERAL PUSHING [*sternly*]. Are you proud of it?

JERRY [*utterly crestfallen*]. Of course, I'm proud of it. Don't I look proud? I'm proud as a pecan. [*Resentfully.*] What do you know about it, anyways? You're nothing but a common soldier—I mean a common general.

GENERAL PUSHING [*pityingly*]. I came here to help you, Mr. Frost. [*With warning emphasis.*] Perhaps you are aware that the sovereign State of Idaho is about to ask your resignation.

JERRY [*now thoroughly resentful*]. Look at here, suppose you be the President for a while, if you know so much about it.

GENERAL PUSHING [*complacently*]. I've often thought that what this country needs is a military man at the head of it.

JERRY. All right, then, you just take off that hat and coat!

> *Jerry takes off his own coat. Jones rushes forward in alarm.*

JONES. If there's going to be a fight hadn't we all better go into the billiard-room?

JERRY [*insistently to General Pushing*]. Take off that hat and coat!

GENERAL PUSHING [*aghast*]. But, Mr. President——

JERRY. Listen here—if I'm the President you do what I say.

> *General Pushing obediently removes his sword and takes off his hat and coat. He assumes a crouching posture and, putting up his fists, begins to dance menacingly around Jerry.*
> *But, instead of squaring off, Jerry gets quickly into the General's hat and coat and buckles on the sword.*

JERRY. All right, since you know so much about

being President, you put on my hat and coat and try it for a while.

The General, greatly taken aback, looks from Jerry to Jerry's coat, with startled eyes. Jerry swaggers up and down the lawn, brandishing the sword. Then his eyes fall with distaste upon the General's shirtsleeves.

JERRY. Well, what are you moping around for?

GENERAL PUSHING [*plaintively*]. Come on, Mr. President, be reasonable. Give me that coat and hat. Nobody appreciates a good joke any more than I do, but——

JERRY [*emphatically*]. No, I *won't* give them to you. I'm a general, and I'm going to war. You can stay around here. [*Sarcastically, to Mr. Jones.*] He'll straighten everything out, Mr. Jones.

GENERAL PUSHING [*pleadingly*]. Mr. President, I've waited for this war for forty years. You wouldn't take away my coat and hat like that, just as we've got it almost ready.

JERRY [*pointing to the shirtsleeves*]. That's a nice costume to be hanging around the White House in.

GENERAL PUSHING [*brokenly*]. I can't help it, can I? Who took my coat and hat, anyhow?

JERRY. If you don't like it you can get out.

GENERAL PUSHING [*sarcastically*]. Yes. Nice lot of talk it'd cause if I went back to the War Department looking like this. "Where's your hat and coat, General?" "Oh, I just thought I'd come down in my suspenders this morning."

JERRY. You can have my coat—and my troubles.

Charlotte comes suddenly out of the White House, and they turn startled eyes upon her, like two guilty schoolboys.

CHARLOTTE [*staring*]. What's the matter? Has everything gone to pieces?

GENERAL PUSHING [*on the verge of tears*]. He took my coat and hat.

CHARLOTTE [*pointing to the General*]. Who is that man?

GENERAL PUSHING [*in a dismal whine*]. I'm Major-General Pushing, I am.

CHARLOTTE. I don't believe it.

JERRY [*uneasily*]. Yes, he is, Charlit. I was just kidding him.

CHARLOTTE [*understanding immediately*]. Oh, you've been *nagging* people again.

JERRY [*beginning to unbutton the coat*]. The General was nagging me, Charlit. I've just been teaching him a lesson—haven't I, General?

He struggles out of the General's coat and into his own. The General, grunting his relief and disgust, re-attires himself in the military garment.

JERRY [*losing confidence under Charlotte's stare*]. Honest, everything's getting on my nerves. First it's some correspondence school getting funny, and then *he* [*indicating the General*] comes around, and then all the people out in Idaho——

CHARLOTTE [*with brows high*]. Well, if you want to know what *I* think, *I* think everything's going to pieces.

JERRY. No, it isn't, Charlit. I'm going to fix everything. I've got a firm grip on everything. Haven't I, Mr. Jones? I'm just nervous, that's all.

GENERAL PUSHING [*now completely buttoned up, physically and mentally*]. In my opinion, sir, you're a very dangerous man. I have served under eight Presidents, but I have never before lost my coat and hat. I bid you good morning, Mr. President. You'll hear from me later.

At his salute the fife and drum commence to play. The trio execute about face, and the escort, at three paces, follows the General out the gate.
Jerry stares uneasily after them.

JERRY. Everybody's always saying that I'm going to hear from 'em later. They want to kick me out of this job—that's what they want. They think I don't know.

JONES. The people elected you, Mr. President. And the people want you—all except the ones out in Idaho.

CHARLOTTE [*anxiously*]. Couldn't you be on the safe side and have yourself reduced to Vice-President, or something?

A NEWSBOY [*outside*]. Extra! Extra! Idaho says: "Resign or be Impeached."

JERRY. Was that newsboy yelling something about me?

CHARLOTTE [*witheringly*]. He never so much as mentioned you.

> *In response to Mr. Jones's whistle a full-grown newsboy comes in at the gate. He hands Jerry a paper and is given a bill.*

JERRY [*carelessly*]. Keep the change. It's all right. I've got a big salary.

THE NEWSBOY [*pointing to Jerry's frock coat*]. I almost had one of them dress suits once.

JERRY [*not without satisfaction*]. I got six of them.

THE NEWSBOY. I hadda get one so I could take a high degree in the Ku Klux. But I didn't get one.

JERRY [*absorbed in the paper*]. I got six of 'em.

THE NEWSBOY. I ain't got none. Well, much obliged. So long.

The newsboy goes out.

JONES [*reading over Jerry's shoulder*]. It says: "Idaho flays Treasury choice."

CHARLOTTE [*wide-eyed*]. Does that mean they're going to flay Dada?

JONES [*looking at his watch*]. Senator Fish will be here at any moment now.

CHARLOTTE. Well, all I know is that I'd show some spunk and not let them kick *me* out, even if I *was* the worst President they ever had.

JERRY. Listen, Charlit, you needn't remind me of it every minute.

CHARLOTTE. I didn't remind you of it. I just mentioned it in an ordinary tone of voice.

She goes into the White House. Senator Joseph Fish comes in hesitantly through the gate.

JERRY [*to Jones*]. Here comes the State of Idaho.

FISH [*timorously*]. Good morning, Mr. President. How are you?

JERRY. Oh, I'm all right.

FISH [*hurriedly producing the telegram and mumbling his words*]. Got a little matter here, disagreeable duty. Want to get through as quickly as possible. "Senator Joseph Fish, Washington, D. C. Present the State of Idaho's compliments to President Frost, and tell him

that the people of Idaho demand his immediate resignation." [*He folds up the telegram and puts it in his pocket.*]
Well, Mr. President, I guess I got to be going. [*He moves
toward the gate and then hesitates.*] This was to have
been my wedding-reception day. Of course, Doris will
never marry me now. It's a very depressing thing to
me, President Frost. [*With his hand on the gate latch.*]
I suppose you want me to tell 'em you won't resign,
don't you?

JONES. We won't resign.

FISH. Well, then it's only right to tell you that
Judge Fossile of the Supreme Court will bring a motion
of impeachment at three o'clock this afternoon.

> *He turns melancholy eyes on Doris's window. He
> kisses his hand toward it in a tragic gesture of fare-
> well. Then he goes out.*
> *Jerry looks at Mr. Jones as though demanding encour-
> agement.*

JERRY. They don't know the man they're up against,
do they, Mr. Jones?

JONES. They certainly do not.

JERRY [*lying desperately and not even convincing himself*]. I've got resources they don't know about.

JONES. If you'll pardon a suggestion, I think the
best move you could make, Mr. President, would be to
demand your father's resignation immediately.

JERRY [*incredulously*]. Put Dada out? Why, he used to work in a bank when he was young, and he knows all about the different amounts of money.

A pause.

JERRY [*uncertainly*]. Do you think I'm the worst President they ever had?

JONES [*considering*]. Well, no, there was that one they impeached.

JERRY [*consoling himself*]. And then there was that other fellow—I forget his name. He was *ter*rible. [*Another disconsolate pause.*] I suppose I might as well go down and get a cigar.

JONES. There's just one more man out here to see you and he says he came to do you a favor. His name is—the Honorable Snooks, or Snukes, Ambassador from Irish Poland.

JERRY. What country's that?

JONES. Irish Poland's one of the new European countries. They took a sort of job lot of territories that nobody could use and made a country out of them. It's got three or four acres of Russia and a couple of mines in Austria and a few lots in Bulgaria and Turkey.

JERRY. Show them all out here.

JONES. There's only one. [*He goes into the White House, returning immediately.*]

JONES. The Honorable Snooks, or Snukes, Ambassador to the United States from Irish Poland.

The Honorable Snooks comes out through the swinging doors. His resemblance to Mr. Snooks, the bootlegger, is, to say the least, astounding. But his clothes—they are the clothes of the Corps Diplomatique. Red stockings enclose his calves, fading at the knee into black satin breeches. His coat, I regret to say, is faintly reminiscent of the Order of Mystic Shriners, but a broad red ribbon slanting diagonally across his diaphragm gives the upper part of his body a svelte, cosmopolitan air. At his side is slung an unusually long and cumbersome sword.

He comes in slowly, I might even say cynically, and after a brief nod at Jerry, surveys his surroundings with an appraising eye.

Jones goes to the table and begins writing.

SNOOKS. Got a nice house, ain't you?

JERRY [*still depressed from recent reverses*]. Yeah.

SNOOKS. Wite, hey?

JERRY [*as if he had just noticed it*]. Yeah, white.

SNOOKS [*after a pause*]. Get dirty quick.

JERRY [*adopting an equally laconic manner*]. Have it washed.

SNOOKS. How's your old woman?

JERRY [*uneasily*]. She's all right. Have a cigar?

SNOOKS [*taking the proffered cigar*]. Thanks.

JERRY. That's all right. I got a lot of them.

SNOOKS. That's some cigar.

JERRY. I got a lot of them. I don't smoke that kind myself, but I got a lot of them.

SNOOKS. That's swell.

JERRY [*becoming boastful*]. See that tree? [*The white tree.*] Look, that's a special tree. You never saw a tree like that before. Nobody's got one but me. That tree was given to me by some natives.

SNOOKS. That's swell.

JERRY. See this cane? The band around it's solid gold.

SNOOKS. Is that right? I thought maybe it was to keep the squirrels from crawling up. [*Abruptly.*] Need any liquor? I get a lot, you know, on account of bein' an ambassador. Gin, vermuth, bitters, absinthe?

JERRY. No, I don't. . . . See that sign? I bet you never saw one like that before. I had it invented.

SNOOKS [*bored*]. Class. [*Switching the subject.*] I hear you made your old man Secretary of the Treasury.

JERRY. My father used to work in a——

SNOOKS. You'd ought to made him official Sandy Claus. . . . How you gettin' away with your job?

JERRY [*lying*]. Oh, fine—fine! You ought to see the military review they had for me last week. Thousands and thousands of soldiers, and everybody cheered when they saw me. [*Heartily.*] It was sort of inspiring.

SNOOKS. I seen you plantin' trees in the movies.

JERRY [*excitedly*]. Sure. I do that almost every day. That's nothing to some of the things I have to do. But the thing is, I'm not a bit stuck up about any of it. See that gate?

SNOOKS. Yeah.

JERRY [*now completely and childishly happy*]. I had it made that way so that anybody passing by along the street can look in. Cheer them up, see? Sometimes I come out here and sit around just so if anybody passes by—well, there I am.

SNOOKS [*sarcastically*]. You ought to have yourself covered with radium so they can see you in the dark. [*He changes his tone now and comes down to business.*] Say, you're lucky I found you in this morning. Got the time with you?

Jerry pulls out his watch. Snooks takes it as though to inspect it more closely.

Look here now, Mr. President. I got a swell scheme for you.

JERRY [*trying to look keen*]. Let's hear it.

SNOOKS. You needn't got to think now, just 'cause I'm a hunerd per cent Irish Pole, that I ain't goin' to do the other guy a favor once in a while. An' I got somep'm smooth for you. [*He puts Jerry's watch in his own pocket—the nerve of the man!*]

JERRY. What is it?

SNOOKS [*confidentially*]. Islands.

JERRY. What islands?

SNOOKS. The Buzzard Islands.

Jerry looks blank.

Ain't you neva hearda the Buzzard Islands?

JERRY [*apologetically*]. I never was any good at geography. I used to be pretty good in penmanship.

SNOOKS [*in horror*]. You ain't neva hearda the Buzzard Islands?

JERRY. It's sort of a disagreeable name.

SNOOKS. The Buzzard Islands. Property of the country of Irish Poland. Garden spots. Flowery paradises ina middle of the Atlantic. Rainbow Islandsa milk an' honey, palms an' pines, smellin' with good-smellin' woods and high-priced spices. Fulla animals with million buck skins and with birds that's got feathers that the hat dives on Fifth Avenue would go nuts about. The folks in ee islands—swell-lookin', husky, square, rich, one hunerd per cent Buzzardites.

JERRY [*startled*]. You mean Buzzards?

SNOOKS. One hunerd per cent Buzzardites, crazy about their island, butter, milk, live stock, wives, and industries.

JERRY [*fascinated*]. Sounds sort of pretty, don't it?

SNOOKS. Pretty? Say, it's smooth! Now here's my proposition, an' take it from me, it's the real stuff. [*Impressively*.] The country of Irish Poland wants to sell you the Buzzard Islands—cheap.

JERRY [*impressed*]. You're willing to sell 'em, eh?

SNOOKS. Listen. I'll be fair with you. [*I regret to say that at this point he leans close to Jerry, removes the latter's stick pin and places it in his own tie*.] I've handed you the swellest proposition ever laid before a President since Andrew Jackson bought the population of Ireland from Great Britain.

JERRY. Yeah?

SNOOKS [*intently*]. Take it from me, Pres, and snap it up—dead cheap.

JERRY. You're sure it's a good——

SNOOKS [*indignantly*]. Say, do you think an ambassador would tell you something that ain't true?

JERRY [*"man to man"*]. That's right, Mr. Snooks. I beg your pardon for that remark.

SNOOKS [*touching his handkerchief to his eyes*]. You hurt me, Pres, you hurt me, but I forgive you.

They shake hands warmly.

And now Jerry has an idea—a gorgeous idea. Why didn't he think of it before? His voice literally trembles as he lays his plan before Snooks.

JERRY. Honorable Snooks, listen. I'll tell you what I'll do. I'll—I'll take those Islands and pay—oh, say a round million dollars for them, on one condition.

SNOOKS [*quickly*]. Done. Name your condition.

JERRY [*breathlessly*]. That you'll let me throw in one of the States on the trade.

SNOOKS. What State?

JERRY. The State of Idaho.

SNOOKS. How much do you want for it?

JERRY [*hastily*]. Oh, I'll just throw that in free.

Snooks indicates Mr. Jones with his thumb.

SNOOKS. Get him to take it down.

Jones takes pen in hand. During the ensuing conversation he writes busily.

JERRY [*anxiously*]. The State of Idaho is just a gift, see? But you *got* to take it.

Suddenly the Honorable Snooks realizes how the land lies. He looks narrowly at Jerry, marvelling at an opportunity so ready to his hand.

JERRY [*to Jones*]. Here, get this down. We agree to

buy the Buzzard Islands from the nation of Irish Poland
for one million——

SNOOKS [*interrupting*]. Two million.

JERRY. Two million dollars, on condition that Irish
Poland will also incorporate into their nation the State
of Idaho, with all its people. Be sure and get that,
Jones. With all its people.

JONES. I have it. The State of Idaho and four hundred and thirty-one thousand, eight hundred and sixty-
six people. Including colored?

JERRY. Yes, including colored.

SNOOKS [*craftily*]. Just a minute, Pres. This here
State of Idaho is mostly mountains, ain't it?

JERRY [*anxiously*]. I don't know. Is it, Mr. Jones?

JONES. It has quite a few mountains.

SNOOKS [*hesitating*]. Well, now, I don't know if we
better do it after all——

JERRY [*quickly*]. Three millions.

SNOOKS. I'll tell you, I'd like to pull it off for you,
Pres, but you see a State like that has gotta have up-
keep. You take one of them mountains, for instance.
You can't just let a mountain alone like you would a—
a ocean. You got to—to groom it. You got to—to
chop it down. You got to explore it. Now take that
alone—you got to explore it.

JERRY [*swallowing*]. Four millions.

SNOOKS. That's more like it. Now these Buzzard Islands don't require no attention. You just have to let 'em alone. But you take the up-keep on a thing like the State of Idaho.

JERRY [*wiping his brow*]. Five millions.

SNOOKS. Sold! You get the Buzzard Islands and we get five million bucks and the State of Idaho.

JERRY. Got that down, Jones?

SNOOKS. On second thoughts——

JERRY [*in a panic*]. No, no, you can't get out of it. It's all down in black and white.

SNOOKS [*resignedly*]. Awright. I must say, Mr. President, you turned out to be a real man. When I first met you I wouldn't have thought it, but I been pleasantly surprised.

He slaps Jerry heartily on the back. Jerry is so tickled at the solution of the Idaho problem that he feverishly seizes Snooks's hand.

SNOOKS. And even if Irish Poland gets stung on the deal, we'll put it through. Say, you and me ain't politicians, fella, we're statesmen, real statesmen. You ain't got a cigarette about you, have you?

Jerry hands him his cigarette case. Snooks, after taking one, returns the case to his own pocket.

JERRY [*enthusiastically*]. Send me a post-card, Ambassador Snooks. The White House, City, will reach me.

SNOOKS. Post-card! Say, lay off. You and me are pals. I'd do anything for a pal. Come on down to the corner and I'll buy you a cigar.

JERRY [*to Mr. Jones*]. I guess I can go out now for a while.

JONES. Oh, yes.

JERRY. Hang on to that treaty. And, say, when the Secretary of the Treasury wakes up tell him I've got to have five million dollars right away.

JONES. If you'll just come into the office for a moment you can put your signatures on it right away.

Jerry and the Honorable Snooks go into the White House arm in arm, followed by Mr. Jones. Presently Jerry can be seen in the window of the President's office.

A moment later the doors swing open again, this time for the tottering egress of Dada.

Dada, not without difficulty, arranges himself a place in the sun. He is preparing for his morning siesta, and, indeed, has almost managed to spread a handkerchief over his face when in through the gate comes Doris. Her eye falls on him and a stern purpose is born. Dada, seeing her approach, groans in anticipation.

DORIS. Dada, I want to speak to you.

Dada blinks up at her, wearily.

Dada, I want to tell you something for your own good and for Jerry's good. You want Jerry to keep his position, don't you?

DADA. Jerry's a fine boy. He was born to my second wife in eighteen hundred and——

DORIS [*interrupting impatiently*]. Yes, I know he was. But I mean now.

DADA. No, I'll never have any more children. Children are hard to raise properly.

This is aimed at her.

DORIS. Look at here, Dada. What I think is the best thing to do is to resign your position.

DADA. The——?

DORIS. You're too old, you see, if you know what I mean. You're sort of—oh, not crazy, but just sort of feeble-minded.

DADA [*who has caught one word*]. Yes, I'm a little feeble. [*He dozes off.*]

DORIS [*absorbed in her thesis*]. I don't mean you're crazy. Don't get mad. I don't mean you go around thinking you're like Napoleon or a poached egg or anything like that, but you're sort of feeble-minded. Don't you understand, yourself? Sort of simple.

DADA [*waking up suddenly*]. How's that?

DORIS [*infuriated*]. That's *just* the sort of thing I was talking about! Going to sleep like that when a person's trying to tell you something for your own son's good. That's just *exactly* what I mean!

DADA [*puzzled but resentful*]. I don't like you. You're a very forward young girl. Your parents brought you up very unsuccessfully indeed.

DORIS [*smugly*]. All right. You're just making me think so more than ever. Go right ahead. Don't mind me. Go right ahead. Then when you begin to really *rave* I'll send for the lunatic-asylum wagon.

DADA [*with an air of cold formality*]. I'll ask you to excuse me. [*He wants to get to sleep.*]

DORIS. First thing you know you'll take all the money in the Treasury and hide it and forget where you put it.

DADA [*succinctly*]. There isn't any money in the Treasury.

DORIS [*after a stunned pause*]. Just what do you mean by that statement?

DADA [*drowsily*]. There isn't any money in the Treasury. There was seven thousand dollars left yesterday, but I worked from morning till night and now there isn't one red penny in there.

DORIS. You must be crazy.

DADA. [*He can scarcely keep awake.*] Hm.

DORIS. Look at here! What do you mean—have you been spending that money—that doesn't belong to you, you know—on some fast woman?

DADA [*as usual, he doesn't quite hear*]. Yes, it's all gone. I went down yesterday morning and I said to myself: "Horatio, you got only seven thousand dollars left, and you got to work from morning till night and get rid of it." And I did.

DORIS [*furious, but impressed at the magnitude of the crime*]. How much was there altogether?

DADA. Altogether? I haven't the figures with me.

DORIS. Why, you old dumb-bell, you. Imagine an old man your age that hasn't had anything to do for twenty years but just sit around and *think*, going crazy about a woman at your age! [*With scornful pity.*] Don't you know she just made a fool of you?

DADA [*shaking his finger at her*]. You must not talk like that. Be courteous and——

DORIS. Yes, and pretty soon some woman comes along and you get "courteous" with her to the extent of all the money in the Treasury.

Jerry now begins to realize that something appalling has indeed happened. He sits down weakly.

DADA. I was working in the dark.

DORIS. Well, Jerry should of had you analyzed in the dark.

JERRY [*suddenly*]. Char-lit!

CHARLOTTE [*at the upper window*]. Stop screaming at me!

JERRY. Charlit, come on out here!

DORIS. Dada's done something awful. At his age!

JERRY. Hurry up out, Charlit!

CHARLOTTE. You wouldn't want me to come out in my chemise, would you?

DORIS. It wouldn't matter. We'll be kicked out, anyways.

CHARLOTTE. Has Dada been drinking?

DORIS. Worse than that. Some woman's got ahold of him.

CHARLOTTE. Don't let him go till I come down. I can handle him.

Mr. Jones comes out.

DADA [*impressively*]. I think the world is coming to an end at three o'clock.

DORIS [*wildly*]. We've got a maniac here. Go get some rope.

MR. JONES [*in horror*]. Are you going to hang him?

Out rushes Charlotte.

DADA. The United States was the wealthiest country in all the world. It's easier for a camel to pass through a needle's eye than for a wealthy man to enter heaven.

They all listen in expectant horror.

So all the money in the Treasury I have had destroyed by fire, or dumped into the deep sea. We are all saved.

JERRY. Do you mean to say that you haven't even got five million dollars?

DADA. I finished it all up yesterday. It was not easy. It took a lot of resourcefulness, but I did it.

JERRY [*in horror*]. But I've got to have five million dollars this afternoon or I can't get rid of Idaho, and I'll be impeached!

DADA [*complacently*]. We're all saved.

JERRY [*wildly*]. You mean we're all lost!

He sinks disconsolately into a chair and buries his face in his hands. Charlotte, who knew everything would go to pieces, stands over him with an "I told you so" air. Doris shakes her finger at Dada, who shakes his finger vigorously back at her. Mr.

Jones, with great presence of mind, produces the cocktail shaker and passes around the consoling glasses to the violently agitated household.

.   .   .   .

.   .   .   .

.   .   .   .

At two-thirty the horizontal sunlight is bright upon the White House lawn. Through the office window the President can be seen, bent over his desk in an attitude of great dejection. And here comes the Honorable Snooks through the gate, looking as if he'd been sent for. Mr. Jones hurries forth from the White House to greet him.

SNOOKS. Did you send for me, fella?

JONES [*excitedly*]. I should say we did, Honorable Snooks. Sit down and I'll get the President.

As Mr. Jones goes in search of the President, Dada comes in through the gate at a triumphant tottering strut. He includes the Honorable Snooks in the splendor of his elation.

DADA [*jubilantly*]. Hooray! Hooray! I worked in the dark, but I won out!

SNOOKS [*with profound disgust*]. Well, if it ain't Sandy Claus!

DADA. This is a great day for me, Mr.— You see the world is coming to an end.

SNOOKS. Well, Sandy Claus, everybody's got a right to enjoy themselves their own way.

DADA. That's in strict confidence, you understand.

SNOOKS. I wouldn't spoil the surprise for nothin'.

Out rushes Jerry.

JERRY [*in great excitement*]. Honorable Snooks—Honorable Snooks——

DADA [*suddenly*]. Hooray! In at the finish.

He tries to slap the Honorable Snooks on the back, but the Honorable Snooks steps out of the way, and Dada loses his balance. Snooks and Jerry pick him up.

JERRY [*suspiciously*]. Dada, have you been drinking?

DADA. Just a little bit. Just enough to fortify me. I never touched a drop before to-day.

SNOOKS. You're a naughty boy.

DADA. Yes, I think I'll go in and rest up for the big event.

He wanders happily into the White House.

JERRY [*in a hushed voice*]. Honorable Snooks, Dada has done something awful.

SNOOKS [*pointing after Dada*]. Him?

JERRY. He took all the money in the Treasury and destroyed it.

SNOOKS. What type of talk is that? You tryin' to kid me?

JERRY. You see, he's a very religious man, Honorable Snooks——

SNOOKS. You mean you ain't got five million for me. [*Jerry shakes his head.*] Good *night!* This is a swell country. A bunch of Indian givers!

JERRY. There's no use cursing at me, Honorable Snooks. I'm a broken man myself.

SNOOKS. Say, can the sob stuff an' call up the Treasury. Get 'em to strike off a couple billion dollars more. You're the President, ain't you?

Cheering up a little, Jerry goes to the telephone.

JERRY. Give me the Treasury Department. . . . Say, this is President Frost speaking. I just wanted to ask you if you couldn't strike off a little currency, see? About—about five million dollars, see? And if you didn't know whose picture to put on 'em you could put my picture on 'em, see? I got a good picture I just had taken. . . . You can't strike any off? . . . Well, I just asked you. . . . Well, I just thought I'd ask you. . . . Well, no harm done—I just *asked* you—it didn't hurt to *ask*, did it? [*He rings off despondently.*] It didn't hurt 'em to *ask*.

SNOOKS. Nothin' doin', eh?

In comes Mr. Jones.

JONES. It's all over, Mr. President. I've just received word that Chief Justice Fossile of the Supreme Court, accompanied by the Senate Committee on Inefficiency, is on his way to the White House.

Jerry sits down, completely overcome. Jones retires.

SNOOKS. They goin' to throw you out on your ear, eh?

JERRY [*brooding*]. It's that low, mean bunch of people out in Idaho.

Snooks, who has been ruminating on the situation, comes to a decision.

SNOOKS. Look at here, Mr. President, I'm goin' to help you out. I'll pass up that five million bucks and we'll make a straight swap of the Buzzard Islands for the State of Idaho.

JERRY [*in amazement*]. You'll give me the Buzzard Islands for the State of Idaho?

Snooks nods. Jerry wrings his hand in great emotion. At this point Charlotte comes out of the White House. At the sight of the Honorable Snooks a somewhat disapproving expression passes over her face.

JERRY [*excitedly*]. Charlit—Charlit. This gentleman has saved me.

CHARLOTTE [*suspiciously*]. Who is he?

JERRY. His name is The Honorable Snooks, Charlit.

SNOOKS [*under Charlotte's stern eye*]. Well, I guess I got to be goin'.

CHARLOTTE. Won't you stay for my husband's impeachment? We're having a few people in.

Out comes Doris, accompanied by Dada. Dada is in such a state of exultation that much to Doris's annoyance he is attempting a gavotte with her.

DORIS [*repulsing him*]. Say, haven't I got enough troubles having to throw over my fiancé, without having you try to do your indecent old dances with me?

Dada sits down and regards the heavens with a long telescope.

Jerry has now recovered his confidence and is marching up and down waving his arms and rehearsing speeches under his breath. Snooks taps Dada's head and winks lewdly at Charlotte and Doris.

DORIS. Honestly, everybody seems to be going a little crazy around here. Is Jerry going to be fired or isn't he?

CHARLOTTE. He says he isn't, but I don't believe him for a minute.

Jones comes out, followed by an excitable Italian gentleman with long, musical hair.

JONES. This gentleman said he had an appointment with Miss Doris.

JERRY. Who are you?

THE GENTLEMAN. I am Stutz-Mozart's Orang-Outang Band. I am ordered to come here with my band at three o'clock to play high-class jazz at young lady's wedding reception.

DORIS. I remember now. I *did* order him. It's supposed to be the best jazz band in the country.

JERRY [*to Stutz-Mozart*]. Don't you know there's going to be a big political crisis here at three o'clock?

DORIS. We can't use you now, Mr. Stutz-Mozart. Anyways, I had to throw over my fiancé on account of political reasons.

STUTZ-MOZART [*indignantly*]. But I have my orang-outang band outside.

CHARLOTTE [*her eyes staring*]. Real orang-outangs?

DORIS. Of course not. They just call it that because they look kind of like orang-outangs. And they play kind of like orang-outangs, sort of. I mean the way orang-outangs would play if they knew how to play at all.

JERRY [*to Stutz-Mozart*]. Well, you'll have to get them away from here. I can't have a lot of senators and judges coming in and finding me with a bunch of men that look like orang-outangs.

STUTZ-MOZART. But I have been hired to play.

JERRY. Yes, but what do you think people would say? They'd say: Yes, here's a fine sort of President we've got. All his friends look sort of like orang-outangs.

STUTZ-MOZART. You waste my time. You pay me or else we play.

JERRY. Look at here. If you're one of these radical agitators my advice to you is to go right back where you came from.

STUTZ-MOZART. I came from Hoboken.

He goes threateningly out the gate.

JONES [*announcing from the steps*]. Chief Justice Fossile of the Supreme Court, accompanied by a committee from the Senate!

CHARLOTTE [*to Jerry*]. Speak right up to them. Show them you're not just a vegetable.

Here they come! Chief Justice Fossile, in a portentous white wig, is walking ponderously at the head of the procession. Five of the six Senators who follow him are large, grave gentlemen whose cutaway coats press in their swollen stomachs. Beside them Senator Fish seems frail and ineffectual.

The delegation comes to a halt before Jerry, who regards it defiantly, but with some uneasiness.

JUDGE FOSSILE. To the President of the United States—greetings.

JERRY [*nervously*]. Greetings yourself.

Mr. Jones has provided chairs, and the Senators seat themselves in a row, with Judge Fossile in front. Fish looks miserably at Doris. The Honorable Snooks lurks in the shadow of the Special Tree.

JUDGE FOSSILE. Mr. President, on the motion of the gentleman from Idaho—[*He points to Fish, who tries unsuccessfully to shrink out of sight.*] we have come to analyze you, with a view to impeachment.

JERRY [*sarcastically*]. Oh, is that so? [*He looks for encouragment at Charlotte. Charlotte grunts.*]

JUDGE FOSSILE. I believe that is the case, Senator Fish?

FISH [*nervously*]. Yes, but personally I like him.

CHARLOTTE. Oh, you do, do you? [*She nudges Jerry.*] Speak right up to them like that.

JERRY. Oh, you do, do you?

JUDGE FOSSILE. Remove that woman!

No one pays any attention to his request.

JUDGE FOSSILE. Now, Mr. President, do you absolutely refuse to resign on the request of the Senator from Idaho?

JERRY. You're darn right I refuse!

JUDGE FOSSILE. Well, then, I——

At this point Mr. Stutz-Mozart's Orang-Outang Band outside of the wall launches into a jovial jazz rendition of "Way Down upon the Suwanee River." Suspecting it to be the national anthem, the Senators glance at each other uneasily, and then, removing their silk hats, get to their feet, one by one. Even Judge Fossile stands at respectful attention until the number dies away.

JERRY. Ha-ha! That wasn't "The Star-Spangled Banner."

The Senators look confused.

DORIS [*tragically*]. This was to have been my wedding reception day.

Senator Fish begins to weep softly to himself.

JUDGE FOSSILE [*angrily to Jerry*]. This is preposterous, sir! You're a dangerous man! You're a menace to the nation! We will proceed no further. Have you anything to say before we vote on the motion made by the State of Idaho?

CHARLOTTE. Yes, he has. He's got a whole mouthful!

DORIS. This is the feature moment of my life. Cecil B. Demille would shoot it with ten cameras.

JUDGE FOSSILE. Remove these women.

The women are not removed.

JERRY [*nervously*]. Gentlemen, before you take this step into your hands I want to put my best foot forward. Let us consider a few aspects. For instance, for the first aspect let us take, for example, the War of the Revolution. There was ancient Rome, for example. Let us not only live so that our children who live after us, but also that our ancestors who preceded us and fought to make this country what it is!

   General applause.

And now, gentlemen, a boy to-day is a man to-morrow —or, rather, in a few years. Consider the winning of the West—Daniel Boone and Kit Carson, and in our own time Buffalo Bill and—and Jesse James!

   Prolonged applause.

Finally, in closing, I want to tell you about a vision of mine that I seem to see. I seem to see Columbia— Columbia—ah—blindfolded—ah—covered with scales— driving the ship of state over the battle-fields of the republic into the heart of the golden West and the cotton-fields of the sunny South.

   Great applause. Mr. Jones, with his customary thoughtfulness, serves a round of cocktails.

JUDGE FOSSILE [*sternly*]. Gentlemen, you must not let yourselves be moved by this man's impassioned rhetoric.

The State of Idaho has moved his impeachment. We shall put it to a vote——

JERRY [*interrupting*]. Listen here, Judge Fossile, a state has got to be part of a country in order to impeach anybody, don't they?

JUDGE FOSSILE. Yes.

JERRY. Well, the State of Idaho doesn't belong to the United States any more.

A general sensation. Senator Fish stands up and sits down.

JUDGE FOSSILE. Then who does it belong to?

SNOOKS [*pushing his way to the front*]. It belongs to the nation of Irish Poland.

An even greater sensation.

JERRY. The State of Idaho is nothing but a bunch of mountains. I've traded it to the nation of Irish Poland for the Buzzard Islands.

Mr. Jones hands the treaty to Judge Fossile.

FISH [*on his feet*]. Judge Fossile, the people of Idaho——

SNOOKS. Treason! Treason! Set down, fella! You're a subject of the nation of Irish Poland.

JERRY [*pointing to Fish*]. Those foreigners think they can run this country.

The other Senators shrink away from Fish.

JUDGE FOSSILE [*to Fish*]. If you want to speak as a citizen of the United States, you'll have to take out naturalization papers.

SNOOKS. I won't let him. I'm goin' to take him with me. He's part of our property.

He seizes the indignant Fish firmly by the arm and pins a large "Sold" badge to the lapel of his coat.

DORIS [*heartily*]. Well, I'm certainly glad I didn't marry a foreigner.

Just at this point, when Jerry seems to have triumphed all around, there is the noise of a fife and drum outside, and General Pushing marches in, followed by his musical escort. The General is in a state of great excitement.

GENERAL PUSHING. Mr. President, I am here on the nation's business!

THE SENATORS. Hurrah!

GENERAL PUSHING. War must be declared!

THE SENATORS. Hurrah!

JERRY. Who is the enemy?

GENERAL PUSHING. The enemy is the nation of Irish Poland!

All eyes are now turned upon Snooks, who looks considerably alarmed.

GENERAL PUSHING [*raising his voice*]. On to the Buzzard Islands!

THE SENATORS. Hurrah! Hurrah! Down with Irish Poland!

JUDGE FOSSILE. Now, Mr. President, all treaties are off!

GENERAL PUSHING [*looking scornfully at Jerry*]. He tried to trade the State of Idaho for some islands full of Buzzards. Bah!

THE SENATORS. Bah!

SNOOKS [*indignantly*]. What's ee idea? Is this a frame-up to beat the nation of Irish Poland outa their rights? We want the State of Idaho. You want the Buzzard Islands, don't you?

GENERAL PUSHING. We can take them by force. We're at war. [*To the Senators.*] We've ordered all stuffed Buzzards to be removed from the natural history museums. [*Cheers.*] And domestic Buzzards are now fair game, both in and out of season. [*More cheers.*] Buzzard domination would be unthinkable.

JUDGE FOSSILE [*pointing to Jerry*]. And now, Senators. How many of you vote for the impeachment of this enemy of the commonwealth?

The five Senators stand up.

JUDGE FOSSILE [*to Jerry*]. The verdict of a just nation. Is there any one here to say why this verdict should not stand?

> *Dada, who all this time has been absorbed in the contemplation of the heavens, suddenly throws down his telescope with a crash.*

DADA [*in a tragic voice*]. It's too late!

ALL. Too late?

DADA. Too late for the world to end this afternoon. I must have missed the date by two thousand years. [*Wringing his hands.*] I shall destroy myself!

> *Dada tries to destroy himself. He produces a pistol, aims at himself, and fires. He flounders down— but he has missed.*

DORIS [*standing over him and shaking her finger*]. You miss *everything*! I'm going to send for the lunatic-asylum wagon—if it'll *come!*

DADA [*shaking his finger back at her*]. Your parents brought you up very unsuccessfully——

JUDGE FOSSILE. Silence! I will pronounce sentence of impeachment on this enemy of mankind. Look upon him!

> *They all look dourly at Jerry.*

Now, gentlemen, the astronomers tell us that in the far

heavens, near the southern cross, there is a vast space called the hole in the sky, where the most powerful telescope can discover no comet nor planet nor star nor sun.

They all look very cold and depressed. Jerry shivers. Fish picks up Dada's abandoned telescope and begins an eager examination of the firmament.

In that dreary, cold, dark region of space the Great Author of Celestial Mechanism has left the chaos which was in the beginning. If the earth beneath my feet were capable of expressing its emotions it would, with the energy of nature's elemental forces, heave, throw, and project this enemy of mankind into that vast region, there forever to exist in a solitude as eternal as—as eternity.

When he finishes a funereal silence falls.

JERRY [*his voice shaken with grief*]. Well, Judge, all I've got to say is that no matter what you'd done I wouldn't want to do all those things to you.

JUDGE FOSSILE [*thunderously*]. Have you anything more to say?

JERRY [*rising through his defeat to a sort of eloquent defiance*]. Yes. I want to tell you all something. I don't want to be President. [*A murmur of surprise.*] I never asked to be President. Why—why, I don't even know how in hell I ever *got* to be President!

GENERAL PUSHING [*in horror*]. Do you mean to say that there's one American citizen who does not desire the sacred duty of being President? Sir, may I ask, then, just what you do want?

JERRY [*wildly*]. Yes! I want to be left alone.

> *Outside the wall Mr. Stutz-Mozart's Orang-Outang Band strikes up "The Bee's Knees." The Senators arise respectfully and remove their hats, and General Pushing, drawing his sword, stands at the salute.*
>
> *Four husky baggage smashers stagger out of the White House with the trunks of the Frost family, and hurry with them through the gate. Half a dozen assorted suitcases are flung after the trunks.*
>
> *The music continues to play, the Senators continue to stand. The Frost family gaze at their departing luggage, each under the spell of a different emotion. Charlotte is the first to pick up her grip. As she turns to the Senators, the music sinks to pianissimo, so her words are distinctly audible.*

CHARLOTTE. If it's any satisfaction to you, I'm going to be a different wife to him from now on. From now on I'm going to make his life perfectly miserable.

> *Charlotte goes out to a great burst of jazz. Dada, with some difficulty, locates his battered carpet-bag.*

DADA. I find I missed the date by two thousand years. Eventually I will destroy myself.

Dada is gone now, hurried out between two porters, and Doris is next. With dignity she selects her small but arrogant hand-bag.

DORIS. All I want to say is if Cecil B. Demille ever saw the White House he'd say: "All right, that may do for the gardener's cottage. Now I'll start building a *real* house."

As she leaves she tries desperately to walk out of step with the music and avoid the suggestion of marching. The attempt is not altogether successful. President Jerry Frost now picks up his bag.

JERRY [*defiantly*]. Well, anyways I showed you you couldn't put anything over on me. [*Glancing around, his eye falls on the "Special Tree." He goes over and pulls it up by the roots.*] This was given to me by some natives. That sign's mine, too. I had it invented. [*He pauses.*] I guess you think I wasn't much good as a President, don't you? Well, just try electing me again.

GENERAL PUSHING [*sternly*]. We won't! As a President you'd make a good postman.

At this sally there is a chorus of laughter.
Then Charlotte's voice again. Does it come from outside the gate, or, mysteriously enough, from somewhere above?

CHARLOTTE [*very distinctly*]. Shut the door! I can smell that stuff up here!

> *A bewildered look comes into Jerry's eyes. He says "What?" in a loud voice.*
>
> *Then with the tree in one hand and his grip in the other, he is hurried, between two porters, briskly toward the gate, while the Orang-Outang Band crashes into louder and louder jazz and*

THE CURTAIN FALLS

ACT III

Now we're back at the Frosts' house, and it's a week after the events narrated in Act I. It is about nine o'clock in the morning, and through the open windows the sun is shining in great, brave squares upon the carpet. The jars, the glasses, the phials of a certain memorable night have been removed, but there is an air about the house quite inconsistent with the happy day outside, an air of catastrophe, a profound gloom that seems to have settled even upon the "Library of Wit and Humor" in the dingy bookcase.

There is brooding going on upon the premises.

A quick tat-tat-tat from outdoors—the clatter of someone running up the porch steps. The door opens and Doris comes in, Doris in a yellowish skirt with a knit jersey to match, Doris chewing, faintly and delicately, what can surely be no more than a sheer wisp of gum.

DORIS [*calling*].   Char-lotte.

A VOICE [*broken and dismal, from up-stairs*].   Is that you, Doris?

DORIS.   Yeah.   Can I come up?

THE VOICE. [*It's Charlotte's. You'd scarcely have recognized it.*] I'll come down.

DORIS. Heard anything from Jerry?

CHARLOTTE. Not a word.

Doris regards herself silently, but with interest, in a small mirror on the wall. In comes Charlotte—and oh, how changed from herself of last week. Her nose and eyes are red from weeping. She's chastened and depressed.

DORIS [*with cheerful pessimism*]. Haven't heard a word, eh?

CHARLOTTE [*lugubriously*]. No. Not one.

DORIS [*impressed in spite of herself*]. Son of a gun! And he sneaked away a week ago to-night.

CHARLOTTE. It was that awful liquor, I *know*. He sat up all night and in the morning he was gone.

DORIS. It's the funniest thing I ever heard of, his sneaking off this way. . . . Say, Charlotte, I've been meaning to say something to you for a couple of days, but I didn't want to get you depressed.

CHARLOTTE. How could I possibly be any more depressed than I am?

DORIS. Well, I just wanted to ask you if you'd tried the morgue yet. [*Charlotte gives a little scream.*] Wait a minute. Get control of yourself. I simply think you ought to *try* it. If he's anywhere you ought to locate him.

CHARLOTTE [*wildly*]. Oh, he's not dead! He's not dead!

DORIS. I didn't say he was, did I? I didn't say he was. But when a fella wanders out tight after drinking some of this stuff, you can't tell *where* you'll find him. Let me tell you, Charlotte, I've had more experience with this sort of thing than you have.

CHARLOTTE. The detective is coming to report this morning.

DORIS. Has he been combing the dives? You ought to have him comb the dives, Charlotte. I saw a picture last week that ought to be a lesson to any woman that loses her husband in a funny way like this. The woman in this picture lost her husband and she just combed the dives and—there he was.

CHARLOTTE [*suspiciously*]. What was he doing?

DORIS. Some vampire was sitting on his lap in a café. [*Charlotte moans.*] But it does show that if you do have the dives combed, you can find 'em. That's what this woman did. . . . There's where most men go when they wander out like that.

CHARLOTTE. Oh, no, Jerry wouldn't go to the dives, or the—the morgue, either. He's never drank or done anything like that till that night. He's always been so mild and patient.

This is a new note from Charlotte.

DORIS [*after a thoughtful pause*]. Maybe he's gone to Hollywood to go in the movies. They say a lot of lost men turn up there.

CHARLOTTE [*brokenly*]. I don't know what to do. Maybe I'm re-responsible. He said that night he might have been P-President if it hadn't been for me. He'd just been analyzed, and they found he was per-perfect.

DORIS. Well, with no reflections on the dead or anything like that, Charlotte, he wasn't so wonderful as you make out. You can take it from me, he never would have been anything more than a postman if you hadn't made him be a railroad clerk. . . . I'd have the dives combed.

CHARLOTTE [*eulogistically*]. He was a good husband.

DORIS. You'll get over it.

CHARLOTTE. What?

DORIS. Cheer up. In a year or so you'll never know you ever had a husband.

CHARLOTTE [*bursting into tears at this*]. But I want him back.

DORIS [*reminiscently*]. Do you know the song? Do you know the song? [*She sings:*]

"A good man is hard to find
    You always get the other kind
    And when you think that he is your friend
    You look around and find him scratching
    'Round some other hen——"

*She has forgotten her ethical connection and begins to
enjoy the song for itself, when Charlotte interrupts.*

CHARLOTTE [*in torture*]. Oh, don't! Don't!

DORIS. Oh, excuse me. I didn't think you'd take it
personally. . . . It's just about colored people.

CHARLOTTE. Oh, do you suppose he's with some
colored women?

DORIS [*scornfully*]. No-o-o! What you need is to
get your mind off it for a while. Just say to yourself
if he's in a dive, he's in a dive, and if he's in Hollywood, he's in Hollywood, and if he's in the morgue——

CHARLOTTE [*frantically*]. If you say that word again.
I'll go crazy!

DORIS. —well, in that *place*, then, just say: "I can't
do anything about it, so I'm going to forget it." That's
what you want to say to yourself.

CHARLOTTE. It's easy enough to *say*, but I can't get
my mind——

DORIS. Yes, you can. [*Magnanimously.*] I'll tell

you about what I've been doing. I've had sort of a scrap with Joseph.

CHARLOTTE. Joseph who?

DORIS. Joseph Fish. He's that fella I brought around here, only you didn't meet him. I told you about him. The one I got engaged to about ten days ago. His parents were in the mortuary business.

CHARLOTTE. Oh.

DORIS. Well, I been trying to make him stop chewing gum. I offered to give it up if he would. I think it's sort of common when two people that go together are always whacking away at a piece of gum, don't you?

There's a ring at the door-bell.

CHARLOTTE. That's the detective.

DORIS [*prudently*]. Have you got that liquor hidden?

CHARLOTTE. I threw that horrible stuff away. Go let him in.

Charlotte goes to the door and ushers in the detective. The detective wears an expression of profound sagacity upon his countenance.

Have you found him?

THE DETECTIVE [*impressively*]. Mrs. Frost, I think so.

CHARLOTTE. Alive?

THE DETECTIVE. Alive.

CHARLOTTE. Where is he?

THE DETECTIVE. Wait. Be calm. I've had several clews, and I've been following them up one at a time. And I've located a man, who answers to the first name of Jerry, that I think is your husband.

CHARLOTTE. Where did you find him?

THE DETECTIVE. He was picked up trying to jimmy his way into a house on Crest Avenue.

CHARLOTTE. Good heavens!

THE DETECTIVE. Yep—and his name is Jerry. He had it tattooed on his arm.

CHARLOTTE. Good God!

THE DETECTIVE. But there's one thing that's different from your description. What color is your husband's hair?

CHARLOTTE. Brown.

THE DETECTIVE. Brown? Are you sure?

CHARLOTTE. Am I sure? Of course I'm sure.

THE DETECTIVE [to Doris]. Do you collaborate that?

DORIS. When he left here it was brown.

THE DETECTIVE. Well, this fella's hair was red.

CHARLOTTE. Oh, it's not Jerry then—it's not Jerry.

DORIS [to Charlotte]. Well, now, how do you know?

Maybe— [*She turns to the detective.*] You see, this fella had been drinking some of this funny liquor you get around here sometimes and it may just have turned his hair red.

CHARLOTTE [*to the detective*]. Oh, do you think so?

THE DETECTIVE. I never heard of a case like that. I knew a fella whose hair was turned white by it.

DORIS. I knew one, too. What was the name of the fella you knew?

CHARLOTTE. Did this man claim to be my husband?

THE DETECTIVE. No, madam, he didn't. He said he had two wives out in Montana, but none that he knew of in these parts. But of course he may have been bluffing.

DORIS. It doesn't sound like Jerry to me.

THE DETECTIVE. But you can identify him by that tattoo mark.

CHARLOTTE [*hastily*]. Oh, he never had one.

THE DETECTIVE. Are you sure?

CHARLOTTE. Oh, yes.

THE DETECTIVE [*his face falling*]. Well, then, he's not our man, because this fella's tattoo marks are three years old. Well, that's a disappointment. That's a great disappointment for me. I've wasted some time over this man. I'd been hoping he'd—ah—do.

CHARLOTTE [*hastily*]. Oh, no, he wouldn't do at all. I'll have to have the right man or I won't pay you.

THE DETECTIVE. Well, now then, I've been following up another clew. Did your husband ever have aphasia?

CHARLOTTE. Oh, no, he's always been very healthy. He had some skin trouble about——

DORIS. He doesn't mean that, Charlotte. Aphasia's where a man runs off and commits murder and falls in love with a young girl under another name.

CHARLOTTE. Oh, no, he's never done anything like this ever before.

THE DETECTIVE. Suppose you tell me exactly what did happen.

CHARLOTTE. Well, I told you he'd been drinking something that had spirits of nitrogen in it.

THE DETECTIVE. Spirits of nitrogen!

CHARLOTTE. That's what the man said. It was sympathetic gin that this man had persuaded Jerry into buying.

THE DETECTIVE. Yes.

CHARLOTTE. And he'd been talking all evening about all the things he could have done if I hadn't stood in his way. He had some examination he'd just taken.

DORIS [*explaining*]. A psychical examination.

THE DETECTIVE [*wisely*]. I see.

CHARLOTTE. And my sister came over with the man she's going to marry, and she came up to see me, and when she came down Jerry was asleep in his chair. Well, I didn't go down. I wish I had now. And my sister here and her fellow went away. Then I went to bed, and it seems to me I could hear Jerry talking to himself in his sleep all night. I woke up about twelve, and he was saying something loud, and I told him to shut the door, because I could smell that awful sympathetic gin way up-stairs.

THE DETECTIVE. Yes.

CHARLOTTE. And that's all. When I came down next morning at seven, he was gone.

THE DETECTIVE [*rising*]. Well, Mrs. Frost, if your man can be located, I'm going to locate him.

DORIS. Have you thought of combing the dives?

THE DETECTIVE. What?

DORIS. Have you combed the dives? It seems to me that I'd make the rounds of all the dives, and I wouldn't be a bit surprised if you'd see this man with somebody sitting on his knee.

THE DETECTIVE [*to Charlotte*]. Does he run to that?

CHARLOTTE [*hurriedly*]. Oh, no. Oh, no.

DORIS [*to Charlotte*]. How do you know?

A brisk knock at the door. Doris opens it eagerly, admitting a small, fat, gray-haired man in a state of great indignation.

THE DETECTIVE [*to Charlotte*]. Is this the pursued?

THE MAN [*sternly*]. You are speaking to Mr. Pushing. I employ or did employ the man who lives in this house.

CHARLOTTE [*wildly*]. Oh, where is he?

MR. PUSHING. That's what I came here to find out. He hasn't been at work for a week. I'm going to let him go.

DORIS. You ought to be ashamed of yourself. He may be dead.

MR. PUSHING. Dead or alive, he's fired. I had him analyzed. He didn't have any ambition, and my analyzer gave him nothing but a row of goose-eggs. Bah!

CHARLOTTE. I don't care. He's mine.

DORIS [*correcting her*]. "Was" mine.

THE DETECTIVE. Maybe you could tell me something about his habits in business hours.

MR. PUSHING. If you'll come along with me I'll show you his analyzed record. We're having it framed. [*Contemptuously.*] Good morning.

He goes out. The Detective, after a nod at Charlotte and Doris, follows him.

DORIS. Well, I should think you'd be encouraged.

CHARLOTTE. Why?

DORIS. Well, that detective found a fella that's something like him. The same first name, anyway. That shows they're getting warm.

CHARLOTTE. Somehow it doesn't encourage me.

Uncertain steps on the stairs. Dada appears wearing a battered hat and carrying a book under his arm.

DORIS. Hello, Dada. Where you going?

DADA [*hearing vague words*]. Hm.

CHARLOTTE. He's going down to the library.

DADA [*in spirited disagreement*]. No. You were wrong that time. I'm not going to the park. I'm going to the library.

DORIS [*sternly*]. Where do you think your son is?

DADA. The——?

DORIS [*louder*]. Where do you think Jerry is, by this time?

DADA [*to Charlotte*]. Didn't you tell me he was away?

Charlotte nods drearily.

DADA [*placidly*]. Hasn't come back yet?

DORIS. No. We're having the dives combed.

DADA. Well, don't worry. I remember I ran away

from home once. It was in 1846. I wanted to go to Philadelphia and see the Zoo. I tried to get home, but they took me and locked me up.

DORIS [*to Charlotte*]. In the monkey house, I bet.

DADA. [*He missed this, thank God!*] Yes, that's the only time I ever ran away.

DORIS. But this is a more serious thing, Dada.

DADA. Boys will be boys. . . . Well, it looks like a nice day.

CHARLOTTE [*to Doris*]. He doesn't care. He doesn't even understand what it's all about. When the detective searched his bedroom he thought it was the plumber.

DORIS. He understands. Sure you do, don't you, Dada? You understand what it's all about, don't you, Dada?

DADA [*aggravatingly*]. The——?

CHARLOTTE. Oh, let him go. He makes me nervous.

DORIS. Maybe he could think out some place where Jerry's gone. He's supposed to *think* so much.

DADA. Well, good afternoon. I think I'll go down to the library. [*Dada goes out by the front door.*]

DORIS. Listen, Charlotte. I was going to tell you about Joseph—to get your mind off yourself, don't you remember?

CHARLOTTE. Yes.

DORIS. I've gotten sort of tired of him. Honestly, I ought to get myself psychoanalyzed.

CHARLOTTE. Why don't you throw him over then? You ought to know how by this time.

DORIS. Of course, having been unlucky in your own marriageable experience, you aren't in a position to judge what I should do.

CHARLOTTE. Do you love him?

DORIS. Well, not—not especially.

CHARLOTTE. Then throw him over.

DORIS. I would—except for one thing. You see, it'd be sort of hard.

CHARLOTTE. No, it wouldn't.

DORIS. Yes, it would. It wouldn't be any cinch.

CHARLOTTE. Why?

DORIS. Well, you see I've been married to him for three days.

CHARLOTTE [astounded]. What!

DORIS. That isn't very long, but you see in marriage every day counts.

CHARLOTTE. Well, then, you can't throw him over.

DORIS. It's next to impossible, I guess.

CHARLOTTE. Was it a secret marriage?

DORIS. Yes, there was nobody there but I and Joseph and the fella that did it. And I'm still living at home. You see, this girl that Joe was keeping waiting to see whether he was going to marry me or not, got impatient, and said she couldn't be kept waiting any longer. It made her sort of nervous. She couldn't eat her meals.

CHARLOTTE. So you got married. And now you're tired of him.

DORIS. No, not exactly that, but it just sort of makes me uncomfortable, Charlotte, to know that you can't throw over the man you've got without causing a lot of talk. Suppose he took to drink or something. You know everybody can't get rid of their husbands as easy as you did.

CHARLOTTE. One husband was always enough for me.

DORIS. One may be all right for you, Charlotte, because you're a monographist, but supposing Rodolph Valentino, or the Prince of Wales, or John D. Rockefeller was to walk in here and say: "Doris, I've worshipped you from a distance on account of the picture that you sent to the fame and fortune contest of the movie magazine, that got left out by accident or lost or something. Will you marry me?" What would you say, Charlotte?

CHARLOTTE. I'd say no. I'd say, give me back Jerry.

DORIS. Would you let having a husband stand in

the way of your life's happiness? I tell you I wouldn't.
I'd say to Joe: "You run up to the store and buy a bag
of peanuts and come back in about twenty years." I
would, Charlotte. If I could marry Douglas Fairbanks
I'd get rid of Joseph in some peaceful way if I *could*—
but if I couldn't I'd give him some glass cough-drops
without a minute's hesitation.

CHARLOTTE [*horrified*]. Doris!

DORIS. And I told Joseph so, too. This marriage
business is all right for narrow-minded people, but I like
to be where I can throw over a fella when it gets to be
necessary.

CHARLOTTE. If you had Jerry you wouldn't feel that
way.

DORIS. Why, can't you see, Charlotte, that's the
way Jerry must have felt?

Charlotte, overcome, rises to go.

And, Charlotte, I don't want to depress you, but if he
is—if it turns out that he is in the mor—in that place—
I know where you can get some simply *stunning* mourn-
ing for——

Charlotte begins to weep.

Why, what's the matter? I just thought it'd cheer you
up to know you could get it cheap. You'll have to
watch your money, you know.

Charlotte hurries from the room.

DORIS. I wonder what's the matter with her.

JOSEPH FISH [*outside*]. Oh, Doris!

Doris goes to the window.

DORIS. How did you know I was here?

FISH [*outside*]. They told me at your house. Can I come in?

DORIS. Yes, but don't holler around so. Haven't you got any respect for the missing?

Fish comes in.

FISH. Doris, I'm awfully sorry about——

DORIS. Oh, Joseph, haven't you got any sense? Sitting there last night everything was perfect, and just when I was feeling sentimental you began talking about embalming—in the *twi*light. And I was just about to take out my removable bridge. . . .

FISH. I'm sorry. . . . Have they found your sister's husband yet?

DORIS. No.

FISH. Has he gone away permanently? Or for good?

DORIS. We don't know. We're having the dives combed. Listen, has any one in your family ever had aphasia?

FISH. What's that?

DORIS. Where you go off and fall in love with girls and don't know what you're doing.

FISH. I think my uncle had that.

DORIS. Sort of dazed?

FISH. Well, sort of. When there was any women around he got sort of dazed.

DORIS [*thoughtfully*]. I wonder if you could inherit a thing from your uncle. [*She removes her gum secretly.*] What are you chewing, Joe?

FISH. Oh, just an old piece of something I found in my mouth.

DORIS. It's gum. I thought I asked you not to chew gum. It doesn't look clean-cut for a man to be chewing gum. You haven't got any sense of what's nice, Joseph. See here, suppose I was at a reception and went up to Mrs. Astor or Mrs. Vanderbilt or somebody, like this: [*She replaces her own gum in her mouth —she needs it for her imitation.*] How do you do, Mrs. Vanderbilt? [*Chew, chew.*] What do you think she'd say? Do you think she'd stand it? Not for a minute.

FISH. Well, when I start going with Mrs. Vanderbilt will be plenty of time to stop.

From outside is heard the sound of a metallic whistle, a melodious call in C major.

What's that?

DORIS. Don't ask me.

FISH. It's pretty. It must be some kind of bird.

The whistle is repeated. It is nearer.

There it is again.

Doris goes to the window.

DORIS. It's only the postman.

FISH. I never heard a postman with a whistle like that.

DORIS. He must be a new one on this beat. That's too bad. The old one used to give me my mail wherever I met him, even if he was four or five blocks from my house.

The sound again—just outside the door now.

I'll let him in.

> *She goes to the door and opens it. The figure of the new postman is outlined in the doorway against the morning sky. It is Jerry Frost.*
>
> *But for a particular reason neither Doris nor Joseph Fish recognize him. He is utterly changed. In the gray uniform his once flabby figure appears firm, erect—even defiant. His chin is up—the office stoop has gone. When he speaks his voice is full of confidence, with perhaps a touch of scorn at the conglomerate weaknesses of humanity.*

JERRY. Good morning. Would you like some mail?

DORIS [*taken somewhat aback*]. Why, sure. I guess so.

JERRY. It's a nice morning out. You two ought to be out walking.

FISH [*blankly*]. Huh?

JERRY. Is this number 2127? If it is, I've got a good-looking lot of mail for you.

DORIS [*with growing interest*]. What do you mean, a good looking lot of mail?

JERRY. What do I *mean?* Why, I mean it's got variety, of course. [*Rummaging in his bag.*] I got eight letters for you.

DORIS. Say, you're new on this beat, aren't you?

JERRY. Yes, I'm new but I'm good. [*He produces a handful of letters.*] I'm the best one they ever had.

FISH. How do you know? Did they tell you?

JERRY. No, I just feel it. I know my job. I can give any other mailman stamps and post-cards and beat him with bundles. I'm just naturally *good*. I don't know why.

DORIS. I never heard of a mailman being *good*.

JERRY. They're mostly all good. Some professions anybody can get into them, like business or politics for instance, but you take postmen—they're like angels, they sort of pick 'em out. [*Witheringly.*] They not only pick 'em out—they select 'em.

FISH [*fascinated*].   And you're the best one.

JERRY [*modestly*].   Yes, I'm the best one they ever had. [*He looks over the letters.*] Now here's what I call a clever ad.   Delivered a lot of these this morning. Children like 'em, you know.   They're from the carpet company.

FISH.   Let's see it.   [*He takes the ad eagerly.*]

JERRY.   Isn't that a nice little thing?   And I got two bills for you here.   I'll hide those, though.   Still, maybe you want to clear up all your accounts.   Some people like to get bills.   The old lady next door wanted to get hers.   I gave her three and you'd think they were checks. Anyways, these two don't look very big, from the out-side, anyhow.   But of course you can't tell from the outside.

DORIS.   Let me see them.

FISH.   Let me see them too.

They squabble mildly over the bills.

JERRY.   The thing is for everybody in the house to write what they guess is the amount of the bill on the outside of the envelope, and then when you open the envelope the one who guessed the closest has to pay the bill.

FISH. Or he could get a prize.

JERRY. Something like that. [*He winks at Doris.*] And here's a couple of post-cards. They're sort of pretty ones. This one's—the Union Station at Buffalo.

FISH. Let me see it.

JERRY. And this one says Xmas greetings. It's four months late. [*To Doris.*] I guess these are for you.

DORIS. No, they're for my sister.

JERRY. Well, I haven't read what's written on the back. I never do. I hope it's good news.

DORIS [*inspecting the backs*]. No, they're from an aunt or something. Anything else?

JERRY. Yes, here's one more. I think it's one of the neatest letters I've had this morning. Now, isn't that a cute letter? I call that a cute letter. [*He weighs it in his hand and smells it.*] Smell it.

DORIS. It does smell good. It's a perfume ad.

FISH. Say, that sure does smell good.

JERRY. Well, I've done pretty well by *you* this morning. Maybe you got a letter for me.

DORIS. No, there's none to-day.

JERRY. Funny thing: I came near leaving that pink letter with a little girl down the street who looked as if she needed one pretty bad. I thought that maybe it was really meant for her, and just had the wrong name and address on by mistake. It would of tickled her. I get tempted to leave mail where it really ought to go instead of where it's addressed to. Mail ought to go to people who appreciate it. It's hard on a postman, especially when he's the best one they ever had.

DORIS. I guess it must be.

FISH. Yeah, it must be tough.

They are both obviously fascinated.

DORIS. Well, there's somebody in this house who needs the right letter something *aw*ful. If you get one that looks as if it might do for her you could leave it by here.

JERRY. Is that so? Well, that's too bad. I'll certainly keep that in mind. The next one I think'll do, I'll leave it by here.

DORIS. Thanks.

JERRY. I've got one of these special delivery love-letters for a girl around the corner, and I want to hurry up and give it to her, so as to see her grin when she gets it. It's for Miss Doris——

DORIS [*interrupting*]. That's me. Give it to me now.

JERRY. Sure. Say, this is lucky. [*He starts t. hand it to her.*] Say, listen—why are you like a stenographer?

DORIS. Me?

JERRY. Yes.

DORIS. I don't know. Why?

JERRY. Because I say to you, "Take a letter."

FISH [*wildly amused*]. Ha-ha! Ha-ha-ha!

JERRY [*with some satisfaction*]. That's a good one, isn't it? I made that one up this morning.

FISH. Ha-ha! Ho-ho!

DORIS. Joseph, I asked you to have some respect for the missing. [*To Jerry.*] You see there's a fella missing here and it's his wife that needs the letter.

FISH [*jealously*]. Who's *your* letter from?

DORIS [*reading it*]. It's from my last fiancé. It says he didn't mean to drink the perfume, but the label was off the bottle and he thought it was bay rum.

FISH. My God! Will you forgive him?

JERRY. Don't worry, my boy. Bay rum or perfume, he killed her love with the first swallow. [*He goes toward the door.*] Good-by. I'll try to find that letter for the lady here that needs it so bad.

DORIS. Good-by—and thanks.

FISH. Let me open the door.

> *He opens the door. Jerry goes out. Doris and Fish stare at each other.*

DORIS. Isn't he wonderful?

FISH. He's a peach of a fella, but——

DORIS. I know what you're going to say; that you've seen him somewhere before.

FISH. I'm trying to think where. Maybe he's been in the movies.

DORIS. I think it's that he looks like some fella I was engaged to once.

FISH. He's *some* mailman.

DORIS. The nicest one I ever saw. Isn't he for you?

FISH. By far. Say, Charlie Chaplin's down at the Bijou.

DORIS. I don't like him. I think he's vulgar. Let's go and see if there's anything artistic.

Fish makes an indistinguishable frightened noise.

DORIS. What's the matter?

FISH. I've swallowed my gum.

DORIS. It ought to teach you a moral.

> *They go out. Charlotte comes in drearily. She glances first eagerly, then listlessly at the letters and throws them aside.*
>
> *Clin-ng! The door-bell. She starts violently, runs to open it. It is that astounding product of our constitution, Mr. Snooks.*

CHARLOTTE [*in horror*]. Oh, what do you want?

SNOOKS [*affably*]. Good morning, lady. Is your husband around?

CHARLOTTE. No. What have you done with him, you beast!

SNOOKS [*surprised*]. Say, what's biting you, lady?

CHARLOTTE. My husband was all right until you came here with that poison! What have you done with him? Where is he? What did you give him to drink? Tell me, or I'll scream for the police! Tell me! Tell me!

SNOOKS. Lady, I ain't seen your husband.

CHARLOTTE. You lie! You know my husband has run away.

SNOOKS [*interested*]. Say now, has he? I had a hunch he would, sooner or later.

CHARLOTTE. You made him. You told him to, that night, after I went out of the room! You suggested it to him. He'd never have thought of it.

SNOOKS. Lady, you got me wrong.

CHARLOTTE. Then where is he? If I'm wrong, find him.

SNOOKS [*after a short consideration*]. Have you tried the morgue?

CHARLOTTE. Oh-h-h! Don't say that word!

SNOOKS. Oh, he ain't in the morgue. Probably some Jane's got hold of him. She'll send him home when she gets all his dough.

CHARLOTTE. He isn't a brute like you. He's been kidnapped.

SNOOKS. Maybe he's joined the Marine Corpse. . . . Howsoever, if he ain't here I guess I'll be movin' on.

CHARLOTTE. What do you want of him now? Do you want to sell him some more wood alcohol?

SNOOKS. Lady, I don't handle no wood alcohol. But I found a way of getting the grain alcohol out of iodine an' practically eliminatin' the poison. Just leaves a faint brownish tinge.

CHARLOTTE. Go away.

SNOOKS. All right. I'll beat it.

So he beats it.

Charlotte's getting desperate from such encounters. With gathering nervousness she wanders about the room, almost collapsing when she comes upon one of Jerry's coats hanging behind a door. Scarcely aware of what she's doing, she puts on the coat and buttons it close, as if imagining that Jerry is holding her to him in the brief and half-forgotten season of their honeymoon.

Outside a storm is come up. It has grown dark suddenly, and a faint drum of thunder lengthens into a cataract of doom. A louder rolling now and a great snake of lightning in the sky. Charlotte, lonesome and frightened, hurriedly closes the win-

*dows. Then, in sudden panic, she runs to the
'phone.*

CHARLOTTE. Summit 3253. . . . Hello, this is me.
This is Charlotte. . . . Is Doris there? Do you know
where she is? . . . Well, if she comes in tell her to
run over. Everything's getting dark and I'm frightened. . . . Yes, *may*be somebody'll come in, but *no*-
body goes out in a storm like this. Even the policeman
on the corner has gotten under a tree. . . . Well, I'll
be all right. I'm just lonesome, I guess, and scared. . . .
Good-by.

> *She rings off and stands silently by the table. The
> storm reaches its height. Simultaneously with a
> terrific burst of thunder that sets the windows
> rattling the front door blows open suddenly, letting
> in a heavy gust of rain.*
> *Charlotte is on the verge of hysterics.*
> *Then there is a whistle outside—the bright, mellow
> whistle of the postman. She springs up, clasping
> her hands together. Jerry comes in, covered with a
> rain cape dripping water. The hood of the cape
> partially conceals his face.*

JERRY [*cheerfully*]. Well, it certainly is a rotten day.

CHARLOTTE [*starting at the voice*]. It's awful.

JERRY. But I heard there was a lady here that was

expecting a letter, and I had one that I thought'd do, so no rain or anything could keep me from delivering it.

CHARLOTTE [*greedily*]. A letter for me? Let me have it.

He hands it to her and she tears it open.

It's from Jerry!

She reads it quickly.

JERRY. Is it what you wanted?

CHARLOTTE [*aloud, but to herself*]. It doesn't say where he is. It just says that he's well and comfortable. And that he's doing what he wants to do and what he's got to do. And he says that doing his work makes him happy. [*With suspicion.*] I wonder if he's in some dive. . . . If I wrote him a letter do you think you could find him with it, Mr. Postman?

JERRY. Yes, I can find him.

CHARLOTTE. I want to tell him that if he'll come home I won't nag him any more, that I won't try to change him, and that I won't fuss at him for being poor.

JERRY. I'll tell him that.

CHARLOTTE [*again talking to herself*]. I was trying to nag him *into* something, I guess. Before we were married I always thought there must be some sort of mysterious brave things he did when he wasn't with me. I thought that maybe sometimes he'd sneak away to hunt bears. But when he'd sneak away it was just to roll dice for cigars down at the corner. It wasn't forests—it was just—toothpicks.

JERRY. Suppose that he was nothing but a postman now—like me.

CHARLOTTE. I'll be proud of him if he's a postman, because I know he always wanted to be one. He'd be the best postman in the world and there's something kind of exciting about being the best. It wasn't so much that I wanted him to be rich, I guess, but I wanted him to do something he wouldn't always be beat at. I was sort of glad he got drunk that night. It was about the first exciting thing he ever did.

JERRY. You never would of told him that.

CHARLOTTE [*stiffening*]. I should say I wouldn't of.

Jerry rises.

JERRY. I'll try to get him here at six o'clock.

CHARLOTTE. I'll be waiting. [*Quickly.*] Tell him to stop by a store and get some rubbers.

JERRY. I'll tell him. Good-by.

CHARLOTTE. Good-by.

Jerry goes out into the rain, Charlotte sits down and bows her head upon the table.
Again there are steps on the porch. This time it is Dada, who comes in, closing a dripping umbrella.

DADA [*as one who has passed through a great crisis*].   I borrowed an umbrella from a man at the library.

CHARLOTTE [*in a muffled voice*].   Jerry's coming back.

DADA.   Is he?   A man at the library was kind enough to lend me his umbrella.   [*He goes over to the bookcase and begins an unsuccessful search for the Scriptures. Plaintively*].   Some one has hidden my Bible.

CHARLOTTE.   In the second shelf.

He finds it.   As he pulls it from its place, several other books come with it and tumble to the floor. After a glance at Charlotte, he kicks them under the bookcase.   Then, with his Bible under his arm, he starts for the stairs, but is attracted by something bright on the first stair, and attempts, unsuccessfully, to pick it up.

DADA.   Hello, here's a nail that looks like a ten-cent piece.

He goes up-stairs.   When he is half-way up, there is a sound as if he had slipped back a notch, then silence.

CHARLOTTE [*raising her head*].   Are you all right, Dada?

No answer.   Dada is heard to resume his climb.

Oh, if I could only sleep till six o'clock!

The storm has blown away, and the sun is out and streaming in the window, washing the ragged carpet with light. From the street there comes once again, faint now and far away, the mellow note of the postman's whistle.

CHARLOTTE [*lifting her arms rapturously*]. The best postman in the world!

CURTAIN

The Battle of Buzzard Island

ACT II

SCENE III

S C E N E :   On the Buzzard Islands, at the seat
of war. We're looking at a cross-
section of the opposing trenches -

NO MANS
LAND

and the sentry on the side of Justice
can, after some inspection, be recognized as one DADA, late the Secretary
of the Treasury. Things must be at a
desperate pass indeed when a white
beard is on duty in the front line.
Those creatures with the bodies of
men but the heads and beaks of horrible birds are BUZZARDS! Even with
death around the corner they can be
seen smoking and playing cards and,
from time to time, cursing foully in
their own tongue.

The moon tells you that it's
night -- in fact it's that celebrated
darkest hour which immediately precedes the dawn.

DADA'S uniform is a mass of mud
from boot to collar. HE is completely
fagged out. His attitude is watchful
but horribly dejected and from time

40

Appendix I

The following episodes represent scenes cut from Act II by Fitzgerald during his revisions of the play before its publication in April 1923. His original typescript (Princeton University Library) is here reprinted without any alterations or corrections, except that deleted words or sections are shown in brackets.

The first fragment, "The Musicians," is all that remains of the dream sequence of Jerry Frost as millionaire.

The second fragment, "The Coffin Corner," is a remnant of Act II, Scene 1, which ended with "The Prophecy," the scene from which Fitzgerald drew his original title for the play: *Gabriel's Trombone.*

The remaining two scenes (2 and 3) of the act are represented by "The End of the World" and "The Battle of Buzzard Island." The latter scene is of particular interest since Edmund Wilson felt that Fitzgerald should never have allowed it to be cut. Fitzgerald, too, must have enjoyed this episode, for he illustrated his typescript with a cartoon (see facing page).

THE MUSICIANS

[HORACE

Jest tell you about it tonight, eh?

JERRY

Well, you see, she hasn't exactly told me. But the other day
I sort of saw something -- you know how young people do -- well,
I saw her kissing this young fella, Joseph Salmon, so I knew
they were engaged. And tonight she told me she wanted to speak
to me before I went to bed - so that must be what it's about.

HORACE

Say, that's swell, Mr. Frost.]

JERRY

Like to hear some music?

HORACE

Why, yes, sir.

JERRY

I got some private musicians, you know. (He makes a megaphone
of his hands) Hey! Music! (Immediately three grotesque and
preferably dwarfed musicians come running on the stage, instruments in hand)

JERRY

(sternly) I want to hear some music. What do you like --
sort of sad things? or -- or sort of la-de-da things? (The
three musicians immediately begin to play a gay air)

JERRY

(To Horace) See? If I tell 'em to play they got to play. If
I tell 'em to stop, they stop. Watch. (to the musicians):
Stop! (They do not hear him and continue playing). Stop!
(And finally louder) Hey, you, Stop! Stop! (They stop)
Say, when you're playing and I say to stop, you stop, see?
(The musicians take this browbeating in silence.) Now let's
have something sort of sad. (They play something sad. Jerry
turns to Horace.) Isn't that good? That's supposed to be sad,
you know, sort of sa-a-ad. (He makes a melancholy gesture to
express sadness. The musicians finish) All right, you, that's
enough. [(He throws them some gold coins)] You wait around the
lawn somewhere. I may need you later. You better spend your
time practising up some new pieces. (The musicians go out.
Jerry with a great deal of pride turns to Horace) [Did you see
what I threw them?

HORACE

It looked like twenty dollar gold pieces to me.

JERRY

It was. (Confidentially) You know, that was the smallest

change I had in my pocket? The smallest I had. Most people
have a lot of small change - but I never have anything smaller
than twenty dollar gold pieces - ever. That's funny, isn't
it? Does it surprise you?]

                         HORACE
I'd like to be rich.

                         JERRY
Well, it's very nice. Of course, there's a lot of responsibility. I mean it's a strain on me to have to carry around all
that heavy money. [And of course I have a hard time taking care
of my property. For instance, the railroad wanted to run a line
[spur] through here. I told 'em that if they tried that I'd buy
up the railroad.

                         HORACE
How did you make your money, sir?]

                 *   *   *   *

                  THE COFFIN CORNER

                          [FISH
(blankly) Pick-pick-pick?

                         CHARLOTTE
Yes. Pick-pick-pick!

                          FISH
(in an aggrieved voice) How about me? Would you think
I was going to be married in a week from today? Would you?
I mean by the way Doris acts? I mean pick-pick-pick, like
you said?] (THE TICKER, which has been silent for some time,
begins to rattle off quotations. FISH goes over and reads
the tape)

                          FISH
(gloomily) Fish Coffins have gone to two hundred and
ten and a half. There's going to be a coffin panic, sure.
But I've made a million dollars this morning.

                         CHARLOTTE
(impressed) People never thought of buying coffins when
I was a girl -- unless they were dead, of course.

                          FISH
We showed the American people the psychology of coffin buying.

                         CHARLOTTE
(delicately) There was some -- some little feeling about it
at first, wasn't there?

                              FISH
(warming to his subject) Just at first. But we started
out to put Fish coffins in every home, and we did it. We
got people looking for the Fish labels on their coffins.
We showed them a coffin needn't be an eyesore. We ran ads
showing good-looking girls stepping into cheap but attractive
coffins, and we got testimonials from spirits who had used
Fish coffins.

                           CHARLOTTE
Yes, I was saying I hadn't thought about coffins for years till--

                              FISH
Do you remember our ad that showed the picture of the man that
had ordered his coffin and the one who hadn't?

                           CHARLOTTE)
                           and   )   together
                           FISH   )
One was going like this -- (THEY make a happy face) --
yeah, and the other one was going like this -- (THEY
make a melancholy, harassed face) -- Yeah.

                              FISH
They began to sell like tooth brushes. I don't quite understand it myself. We can't make 'em fast enough. Sometimes
I wonder if a big trust company isn't buying up a billion
dollars worth of coffins for some reason of their own.

                  *   *   *   *

                        THE PROPHECY

                            GENERAL
The End of the world! Why, they can't retire me for five
years yet.

                             DADA
The end of the world is due in the eleventh month of the
administration of my son Jerry by my second wife. (there
is a moment of stunned silence)

                           CHARLOTTE
Well, if you ask me I think it's perfectly morbid!

                            JERRY
Look-at-here, Dada, are you serious about this?

                            DORIS
(utterly convinced and regarding DADA as a major prophet)
What would he buy up all those coffins for if he wasn't serious?

                    FISH
That's true. (HE looks up at the sky and EVERYONE follows
his gaze, rather expecting to see a cloud of glory)

                    JERRY
Well, I've read the evening paper and I didn't see anything
about it.

                    DADA
I've been working in the dark.

                    DORIS
(fascinated) Do you mean you're going to blow up the world?

                    DADA
The world is coming to an end. The last judgment is at
hand. Gabriel's Trump will blow one week from today just at
this hour.

                    FISH
What's a trump?

                    DORIS
It's something like a trombone, only not so good.

                    DADA
The ----?

                    GENERAL
(very depressed) Are you sure it didn't say anything about
a war?

                    DORIS
(loudly) You sure you've got the right day?

                    DADA
Yes. I've got the right day. I've been working on it for
twenty years and finally I calculated it by the second letter
in the third word of every fourth verse of Isaiah. It gave me
Spudmutton, the middle name of my son Jerry by my second wife,
and the date and the hour.

                    JERRY
(convinced) That's my middle name all right.

                    DORIS
(awed) Just think -- it's in the Bible.

                    GENERAL
Well, how about this State of Idaho business?

                    DORIS
(to her new prophet) How about it Dada?

DADA

I've never been there.

CHARLOTTE

Well, I'm going to cancel all my dentist appointments.

JERRY

(jocularly to THE COMPANY at large) Did you ever hear the
story of the two Jews in this wreck --?

CHARLOTTE

This is a fine time to tell stories.

JERRY

Well, it wont hurt anything to tell a story. (HE resumes)
Well, there were two Jews ---- (NO ONE is paying any attention
to him)

FISH

(to DADA) You've got an absolutely straight tip on this,
have you?

JERRY

(trying unsuccessfully -- to attract the attention of first
one person and then another) -- and one of them says, "Now
that the boat's going down, here's that ----"

CHARLOTTE

That's just like you. At a time like this to tell dirty stories!

JERRY

It isn't a dirty story. It's just as clean as it can be!

DORIS

(such beautiful patience) Well, hurry up and get it over then.

JERRY

(the heart taken out of him) Well, he said "Here's that two
dollars I owe you -- Isaac."

CHARLOTTE

(tersely) Go on.

JERRY

That's all there is to it.

DORIS

Well, it isn't very funny.

JERRY

(indignantly) Well, you didn't listen to the first part of
it. You can't hear half a joke and think it's funny. I just
said it was appropriate -- that's the only reason I told it at
all.

DADA
(who misses the Centre of the stage)   This is no time for jokes.

DORIS
(his warmest supporter)   I should say it isn't, Dada.

CHARLOTTE
You're perfectly right!   (THEY ALL look witheringly at JERRY)

JERRY
Oh, let me alone. I guess I can tell a joke when I want to.

DADA
(sententiously)   The President should be warning the people.

DORIS
I'm going to telephone some friends.   (WARWICK goes to the
radio broadcaster)

DADA
I have been trying to think of some way to distribute the coffins.

FISH
Have everybody call for theirs, why don't you?

CHARLOTTE
(dabbing her eyes with her handkerchief)   I don't want the world
to come to an end.

DADA
(indignantly)   It's a good thing that it should.

WARWICK
(talking into the radio)   The President wishes to make an
announcement to the nation of the greatest significance. All
sending stations are to cease broadcasting and give their
attention to --- (HE continues to speak)

DADA
I have provided coffins for a hundred and ninety-two million
people.

FISH
(enthusiastically)   This'll knock the roof off the coffin
market.

WARWICK
(turning around)   We're all ready, Mr. President. I have you
connected with thirty-seven big cities, and stations all over
the country are listening in.   (JERRY mops a glistening brow)

[DORIS
(in rapture)   This is the feature moment of my life. Cecil
B. De Mille would shoot it with ten cameras. (JERRY goes
nervously to the radio)]

                    DORIS
I've got to telephone to some people. (SHE hurries into the
White House)

                    GENERAL
I'll break it to the standing army. (HE hurries off, followed
at a run by his escort who, for once, are not playing)

                    JERRY
(to the radio) Ladies and gentlemen --

                    CHARLOTTE
Couldn't you be a little more pious?

                    JERRY
(to the radio) Couldn't you be a little more pious?

                    DADA
(excitedly) That's right! Don't forget to tell them how I
worked in the dark.

                    JERRY
(still facing the radio) Keep still!

                    FISH
First tell them about the coffin market. (DORIS appears in
the window of JERRY'S office with the telephone in her hand)

                    DORIS
Central, give me Midway 3125.

                    JERRY
(becoming more and more nervous) Dada, my father -- we call
him Dada -- his name is Horatio Frost -- while -- while glancing
through --

                    DORIS
(sticking her head out the window) Where's the telephone
director?

                    JERRY
(into the radio) The telephone directory --

                    DADA
(wildly) No! No! No!

                    JERRY
(into the radio) No!

                    CHARLOTTE
The Bible.

                    JERRY
-- the Bible, discovered --

CHARLOTTE
(sarcastically) Better tell them that joke.

JERRY
There were once two Jews ----

CHARLOTTE
Stop him!

JERRY
(turning around) I thought you said to tell it.

FISH
Go on and say something with some sense to it.

WARWICK
Talk louder, sir.

FISH
Sing something. (CHARLOTTE grows impatient and leaning over
his shoulders shouts into the radio:

CHARLOTTE
The world's coming to an end!

JERRY
(louder and into the radio) That's what I was trying to say!
The world's coming to an end and -----

FISH
(at the ticker) My God! The ticker's busted! Coffins have
hit the sky!

DADA
(piously) Have been carried to the sky.

DORIS
(into the telephone) My dear, don't breathe it to a word --
I mean to a soul. The most hectic thing has happened. Absolutely, my dear. I'm on the point of convulsions ---- (amid
Doris' explanations, JERRY'S nervous shoutings, CHARLOTTE'S
prompting and DADA'S passionate adjurations to tell them how
HE worked in the dark

--THE CURTAIN DESCENDS--

*   *   *   *

THE END OF THE WORLD

[ACT II

SCENE II]

[SCENE:] Still the lawn of the White House, but one week
later -- to the hour, four o'clock. Between the radio and
the gate a wooden scaffolding has been erected. It is about
the height of the garden wall and is evidently to be used as
an observation platform, for a ladder makes it accessible
from the ground.

All serene in the sunshine. Through the gate a policeman can
be seen marching up and down on guard.

The silence is suddenly shattered by the appearance of the
Hon. Snooks who bursts out through the swinging doors of the
White House. The HON. SNOOKS is in a state of considerable
agitation and is hotly pursued by WARWICK)

WARWICK
He's not here -- don't you believe me?

SNOOKS
(suspiciously) Where is he then?

WARWICK
He's saying goodbye to his cabinet. You ought to have better
sense than to come around on a day like this when the whole
world is sitting and waiting for destruction.

SNOOKS
Well, I'm going to wait out here. (HE sits down. MR. WARWICK
glares at him indignantly, and then, taking a slip of paper
from his pocket, goes to the radio)

WARWICK
(at the radio) Four o'clock bulletin. All quiet at the
Capitol. Horatio Frost, Secretary of the Treasury, now known
as the "coffin hero", conducts open air services in Washington
Park. Weather -- (HE inspects the firmament)--fair. (JERRY
comes in through the gate. HE is now dressed in pitch black
clothes and carries a book -- presumably a Bible -- under his
arm. His eye falls with distaste upon the HON. SNOOKS, who
RISES to meet him)

JERRY
(in a hushed voice) Hello, Mr. Snooks.

SNOOKS
Say, what's the idea of all this bunk about the end of the world?

                    JERRY
(<u>reverently</u>) Don't talk so loud. (<u>looking at his watch</u>)
It's due in exactly thirty-five minutes.

                    WARWICK
(<u>showing JERRY a slip of paper</u>) Does the President want me
to send this bulletin you made up?

                    JERRY
All right. Send anything that you can think of.

                    WARWICK
(<u>at the radio</u>) The President and his family will await the
end of the world on the White House Lawn, engaged in prayer
and -- (<u>HE finds difficulty in deciphering a word</u>) -- and
recreation.

                    JERRY
(<u>correcting him</u>) Meditation!

                    WARWICK
(<u>at the radio</u>) Meditation!

                    [SNOOKS
(<u>indignantly</u>) What's ee idea? Is this a frame-up to beat
the nation of Irish Poland outa their rights?

                    JERRY
What rights?

                    SNOOKS
The State of Idaho -- that's their rights. You goin' to get
the Buzzard Islands ain't you?]

                    JERRY
Listen, Mr. Snooks, what you ought to be thinking over is
more serious things. This is supposed to be sort of like
Sunday -- (<u>and HE adds, without humor</u>) -- only worse.

                    SNOOKS
There ain't nothin' more serious to me than gettin' hold of
the State of Idaho like you and me agreed I was goin' to do.
Just because it's ee end of the worl' for youse guys, that
don't mean nothin' to <u>me</u>.

                    JERRY
(<u>sternly</u>) Dada's going to have the end of the world for
everybody. (faint cheering outside/JERRY glances at the sky)

                    SNOOKS
(<u>almost whining</u>) Suppose this big clean-up don't come off,
you ain't goin' to go back on your bargain, are you, Pres.?
(<u>a long burst of cheering outside the wall. DADA comes in
through the gate at a triumphant tottering strut</u>)

DADA

(jubilantly) [Hooray! Hooray! I worked in the dark but I
won out!] Hear them cheering me? I made a great speech.
Thirty thousand people heard me.

JERRY

(to SNOOKS) This is my father, the coffin hero.

DADA

(faintly acknowledging the introduction) Hm. They were faint-
ing so fast that they didn't even stop to carry them out. It
was inspiring. Oh, this is a great day for me!

JERRY

(proudly to SNOOKS) He found out the whole thing, you know.

SNOOKS

If it wasn't for that old goat I'd of got the State of Idaho
like we agreed to.

DADA

I spoke for three hours. Oh, it was wonderful. (SNOOKS
starts off)

JERRY

Where you going? Don't you want to hear about what Dada did?

SNOOKS

No, I rather go get nailed down in my coffin. All I got to
say is if this ain't a straight tip he's got, you better kiss
the State of Idaho goodbye. (HE goes out through the gate)

DADA

The only thing that worries me is to whether everybody's got
a coffin. Except for that I'm happy as a lark.

JERRY

Have you worked out a plan?

DADA

I think they should all sit in their coffins, but I'm not sure.
If it wasn't so late I could look it up in Isaiah.

JERRY

It's after four.

DADA

(enthusiastically) Half an hour more. (HE slaps JERRY on the
back) [Hooray! In at the finish!] (JOSEPH FISH comes in at
the gate)

FISH

(anxiously) Hello, where's Doris?

DADA

Did you hear my speech? I spoke for two hours and over five hundred people fainted. There were fifty thousand people there. It's a great day for us all, eh? [(HE tries to slap FISH on the back, but FISH steps out of the way and DADA loses his balance and falls to the ground. JERRY AND FISH pick him up)

JERRY

(with suspicion) Dada, have you been drinking?]

DADA

[Just a little bit. Just enough to fortify me. I never drank before today, but] I had to speak to a hundred thousand people. So I had just a drop. I spoke for three hours and all but five hundred people fainted. I almost fainted myself, I was so----

FISH

(gloomily) I don't see what you're so happy about.

DADA

You don't! Why the end of the world is coming today! In half an hour---

FISH

Yes, I know all that. But this should of been my wedding day.

DADA

(triumphantly) There shall be no marriage or giving in marriage.

FISH

Say, Mr. Frost, if you're trying to cheer me up I wish you wouldn't say things like that.

DADA

I'll go and tell Charlotte about my speech. I wish my old father had been alive to hear it. He used to say to me, "Horatio-----" (still declaiming, HE goes into the White House)

JERRY

(profoundly) He's a great thinker.

FISH

(gloomily) I suppose so.

JERRY

I always knew he was thinking about something. I never could think things out like that, could you?

                              FISH
You going to eat supper first?

                              JERRY
Sure. (HE hesitates) But I don't suppose it'd be any use,
do you?

                              FISH
Well, we'd have had supper anyways.

                              JERRY
That's right -- and it may be the last meal we'll get for
a long time.

                              FISH
(with a sigh) I was finishing a serial in a magazine. I
don't suppose I ever will know what happened.

                              JERRY
(reassuringly) Sure you will.

                              FISH
Is that a fact?

                              JERRY
Sure, you'll know everything. I'll know who swiped my gold-
filled watch in 1909. (out comes CHARLOTTE, also in black.
The week has made a nervous wreck of her. Her eyes are red
and her cheeks are only the shadows of her skull) Say, Charlit,
are you going to have supper first?

                              CHARLOTTE
Of course not. I couldn't eat a thing.

                              FISH
(consoling her) You wont need anything, Mrs. Frost.

                              CHARLOTTE
(in a wail) I'll be sick I know. I'm always sick when I
go without food.

                              JERRY
Maybe I better have our coffins brought up from the cellar.
I forgot about it.

                              CHARLOTTE
I always said you'd never have a bit of sense till Judgment
Day.

                              JERRY
This is Judgment Day, Charlit.

[CHARLOTTE
(plaintively) Well, you needn't remind me of it every minute.

JERRY
I didn't remind you of it. I just mentioned it in an ordinary
tone of voice.]

FISH
(uneasily) It makes a person feel sort of funny, doesn't it?
I used to think that death was just a matter of coffin quality.

CHARLOTTE
What I want to know is, what's the good of it?

FISH
(with deep melancholy) This was going to have been my wedding
day, Mrs. Frost. (DORIS comes in dressed in an alarming and
astonishing costume, which at a first glance appears to be half
a black smock and half a ballet dress)

DORIS
Hello, people.

FISH
What's that you got on?

DORIS
It's a shroud.

FISH
It looks more like a Hula costume.

DORIS
Well, it isn't, Joseph. It's a shroud. I had it made. I
don't see why a shroud should be depressing. Do you? (ready
for the great journey) Well, when do we start?

FISH
You'd think we were going to Europe, to hear her.

JERRY
(literally) We start in -- twenty minutes. [(WARWICK comes out
of the White House followed by A GENTLEMAN with musical hair.
It is MR. STUTZ-MOZART)

WARWICK
This man says he had an appointment with Miss Doris.]

FISH
(fiercely to STUTZ-MOZART) Are you with a garbage-disposal
service?

[STUTZ-MOZART
Mos' cert'nly not. (to DORIS) Good afternoon. I am here,
as you see, by looking.

JERRY

Who are you?

STUTZ-MOZART

I am Stutz-Mozart's Orangoutang Band. I was tol' to come
here wiz my ban' at five o'clock to play the high-class
Jazz for Mr. Fish's wedding. (THEY ALL look nervously at
their watches)]

FISH

(weakly) It's not five o'clock.

[STUTZ-MOZART

It is quarter to.

DORIS

I remember now. I did order him. It's supposed to be the
best Jazz band in the country.

FISH

(to STUTZ-MOZART) What did you come now for? Don't you know
the world's coming to an end at five o'clock?]

CHARLOTTE

(groping for a chair) I'm going to sit down. I've got
something awful the matter with my knees.

FISH

(with a sickly smile) Let's all get in the house.

DORIS

Dada says we all ought to stay out here.

FISH

How does he know so much about it?

JERRY

He's been working on it twenty years. (THEY are all sitting
down now. MR. WARWICK comes out again) I've got sort of a
stomachache.

WARWICK

(referring to some telegrams in his hand) The doors of the
Salvation Army in Philadelphia are thronged. Thousands are
saved. Associated bootleggers, second biggest industry in
America, goes into the hands of a receiver. Pittsburgh offi-
cials return seven million dollars stolen from the city treasury.

JERRY

See? That's like my story about the two Jews.

CHARLOTTE

If you tell that story again I'll scream. (FISH picks up a spy-glass from the table and regards the heavens)

DORIS

See anything?

FISH

Not a thing.

DORIS

I'll ruin my complexion sitting here without a hat.

FISH

It doesn't matter. You wont need it any more.

DORIS

You needn't be so morbid.

JERRY

Where's Dada?

CHARLOTTE

Yes, where is Dada?

WARWICK

He's asleep in the grand ballroom.

JERRY

Somebody ought to wake him. If he woke up and found he'd missed it he'd never forgive us. (at this point DADA rushes wildly out of the house, even more rumpled than usual)

DADA

Wait for me! Wait for me! ...... (HE looks around, relieved to see that nothing has happened yet) I dozed off to sleep for a moment and when I awoke I thought for a moment I'd been too late. (HE picks up the spy-glass and starts to climb the scaffolding. Several times HE slips back, but finally with the assistance of FISH and WARWICK HE reaches the top -- where HE turns his telescope on the heavens.) (there is a dull mutter of thunder in the distance, and from this point onward the stage grows gradually darker)

FISH

My God!

WARWICK

(at the radio) Five minutes of five. The Secretary of the Treasury mounts to his platform and looks at the sky with a powerful telescope. There is a sound of thunder. (HE turns to JERRY) Do you want to say anything? (JERRY shakes his head, unable to speak) (to the radio) The President is busy

praying for the people. (HE goes to the garden gate and looks
out) There's a big crowd out here looking at the sky and waiting.

                              DORIS
Gosh, this is gloomy! For Heaven's sake somebody tell a story
or something.

                              JERRY
(with a swallow) I started to tell you a story the other day
and ---

                              CHARLOTTE
She means a cheerful story. Something somebody can laugh at.

                              FISH
What time is it?

                              WARWICK
I think a few words over the radio to Congress --

                              JERRY
I don't feel well enough. I've got a sort of stomach ache.
(THEY ALL set their watches)

                              FISH
Will Western time make any difference?

                              JERRY
No, I think they'd go by Eastern time.

                              FISH
It seems to me as if they would anyhow.

                              JERRY
Eastern time's the most important.

                              FISH
Well, about now I suppose everybody's looking for the Fish
label. (DADA drops his telescope and throws them ALL into a
panic)

                              FISH
My God!

                              JERRY
(to WARWICK) Say, scratch my back here, will you? (WARWICK
complies) Higher --- there --- there -- thanks.

                              WARWICK
(with a sudden burst of generosity) Will anybody have a
cigarette?

                    FISH
All right. (but HE looks at his watch) I haven't got time.

                    DORIS
I'm going to count five hundred by fives. Five -- ten --
fifteen -- twenty --

                    CHARLOTTE
(on the verge of collapse) Don't! I can't stand it!

                    DADA
(in a sing-song chant) Get your coffins ready!

                    FISH
What price United Coffins now! (HE is hushed)

                    DORIS
Poke me if I laugh.

                    WARWICK
Half a minute to go. (dead silence falls. The sky has grown
dark and the thunder rolls continuously. Upon the scaffolding
DADA braces himself as if expecting a personal blow. JERRY'S
mouth falls open. HE has a cigar in his hand and several
times HE starts to put it in his mouth, but refrains nervously.
FISH retreats toward the special tree, step by step. DORIS
powders her nose with her eyes fixed on the sky -- but SHE
manages to steal a glance in her mirror).(DADA produces a
pocket flask and takes a small nip, throwing the bottle over
the wall) (another rigid instant ......) (then, at the first
stroke of five there is a mighty uproar! STUTZ-MOZART'S
Orangoutang Band outside the wall has begun to perform --
in a crashing fortissimo) (from EVERYONE on the lawn there
is an immediate response. DADA topples off the platform into
the arms of the unprepared MR. WARWICK -- TOGETHER THEY seek
the White grass. CHARLOTTE rolls from her chair and lies
flat on her back kicking her feet at the inscutable heavens.
FISH begins to rush madly around the stage as if looking for
a way out. DORIS, though frightened, sways from side to side
in a sort of Jazz trance. After a first pandemonium the music
becomes softer, the thunder stops, the sun breaks through the
clouds)

                    DADA
(regaining his feet) The heavenly music! The heavenly music!

                    DORIS
(coming to herself with a start) No! It's Stutz-Mozart's
Orangoutang Band! (THEY look at their watches)

                    FISH
(hardly daring to believe the best) It's two minutes after five!

                          JERRY
(wildly) That's practically impossible!

                        CHARLOTTE
I knew it wouldn't happen. (there is the sound of an angry
mob outside. SNOOKS comes precipitately through the garden
gate. HE eyes the Presidential group with a vindicative glare)

                         SNOOKS
The end of the world, eh? It's the end of the world for Sandy
Claus. You got to come across with the State of Idaho!

                *   *   *   *

              THE BATTLE OF BUZZARD ISLAND

                       [ACT II

                      SCENE III]

[SCENE:] On the Buzzard Islands, at the seat of war. We're
looking at a cross-section of the opposing trenches -- and
the sentry on the side of Justice can, after some inspection,
be recognized as one DADA, late the Secretary of the Treasury.
Things must be at a desperate pass indeed when a white beard
is on duty in the front line. Those creatures with the bodies
of men but the heads and beaks of horrible birds are BUZZARDS!
Even with death around the corner they can be seen smoking and
playing cards and, from time to time, cursing foully in their
own tongue.

The moon tells you that it's night -- in fact it's that celebrated darkest hour which immediately precedes the dawn.

DADA'S uniform is a mass of mud from boot to collar. HE is
completely fagged out. His attitude is watchful but horribly
dejected and from time to time HE gives out a low despairing
noise that lies half between a groan and a sigh. There is no
other sound but the hoarse chirrups from the gambling BUZZARDS
and occasionally a low, portentous booming in the distance.

At length, from what seems to be a dugout in the American
trench, a HUMAN VOICE breaks in upon the dismal scene)

                      [THE VOICE
(anxiously) Is everything all right, Dada?

                         DADA
(gloomily) Hm. Everything but me.

                              THE VOICE
Cheer up, Dada. You're not so old as you feel.

                                DADA
I hope not ...]

                              THE VOICE
(I may as well admit it's JERRY) How's the enemy?

                                DADA
They seem very well.

                                JERRY
I'm coming up now. I've just about finished my digging.
(JERRY emerges from the dugout. HE is, if possible, a little
more muddy than DADA -- his corporal's chevrons are almost
obscured) Have you heard any clucking?

                                DADA
(with a triumphant cackle) I think I shot one of those
Buzzards in the beak awhile ago.

                                JERRY
He'll go without his birdseed for a couple of days, wont he,
[Dada?]

                                [DADA
I'm what you'd consider a dead shot. When I was in the war
of the rebellion General Sheridan used to say to me, "Horatio --"]

                                JERRY
Did you knock his beak off?

                                DADA
I think I managed to dent it pretty bad. But I've got something in my eye.

                                JERRY
That's too bad, Dada. Let's see. (HE approaches DADA and
pulls out a handkerchief) My last clean one. Let's see now --
close the other eye. (HE starts to remove it) Wont it close?
Wont it close? Hold it shut. There, there. Wait a minute,
there. All right I got it.

                                DADA
Did you get it?

                                JERRY
Yes, I got it.

                                DADA
I knew I had something in there. I could feel it.

                    JERRY
Now if you'll just scratch this place right here -- (HE turns
around and offers his back to DADA. DADA scratches it with his
bayonet) Thank you. No, higher. A little lower. Harder.
(hastily) Not so hard! There -- that's fine. Much obliged.
You better stand up there again and keep watch.

                    DADA
(wearily) I think I'm going to have to stand up here forever.

                    JERRY
No you're not, Dada. You wait till you see my scheme. I
got a scheme that's one of the most original schemes that's
ever been tried. (at this point there is the sound of martial
music from the rear and in marches GENERAL COHEN, followed at
three paces by his inevitable fife and drum. JERRY comes to
attention and presents arms. DADA on the contrary pays no
heed whatsoever)

                    GENERAL
(to DADA) Come to attention there.

                    DADA
(engrossed in his own thoughts) Hm. (querulously) Well, you
needn't get so upset about it. I thought you were one of these
Y.W.C.A. fellows. I just shot one of those Buzzards in the beak.

                    JERRY
(confidentially to THE GENERAL) He just thinks he did, General.
He's a little near-sighted.

                    DADA
I heard the sound of the bullet when it hit him in the beak.

                    JERRY
He probably just hit an old tin can.

                    GENERAL
(to JERRY) Are you in command here.

                    JERRY
Yes, sir. [All the officers are killed.]

                    DADA
(helpfully) He was my only boy by my second wife.

                    GENERAL
(after glaring at DADA) Buzzards pretty quiet around here?

                    JERRY
(sententiously) There's only one quiet Buzzard, General, and
that's a dead Buzzard.

GENERAL

That's very good. Very original. The only quiet Buzzard is
a dead Buzzard.

JERRY

General, I got a scheme that'll make them all quiet Buzzards.

GENERAL

Good! Good! Forward it to your Captain.

JERRY

And he can --?

GENERAL

He can forward it to the Colonel.

JERRY

(faintly) I see. and then he can --

GENERAL

He can forward it to me. And I'll consider the matter at the
proper official moment.

JERRY

I've got a lot of schemes. I've got one scheme that'll end
this war in a week.

GENERAL

It's a good war, Corporal. I'm not sure that it's -- ah --
best to end it just yet. The thing is to wea-ear 'em down.
For -- ah -- for my part I've distinctly enjoyed it. (at this
point a rather frightened GENTLEMAN in a frock coat comes
hastily in -- a gentleman easily recognizable as the prosperous
MR. JOSEPH FISH. On seeing the GENERAL a look of relief passes
over his face)

FISH

Oh, there you are, General. I'm Mr. Fish, the coffin magnate.
I've been seeing the rear trenches and I got separated from
my escort.

GENERAL

These are the front line trenches.

FISH

(in deadly terror) My God! Is that a fact? I think the
Buzzards must have realized what a valuable coffin maggot --
magnate -- I am to our government. They've been shooting
cannons at me.

GENERAL

I have to hurry along myself in a minute. I'm dummy in a
bridge game back at headquarters.

[FISH
General, you'll be glad to hear that back home we've ordered
all stuffed Buzzards to be removed from the natural history
museums. And domestic Buzzards are now fair game both in and
out of season.

                              GENERAL
(sternly) Buzzard domination would be unthinkable.]

                               FISH
(ferociously, to JERRY) Bayonet one for me. Will you?

                              JERRY
(taken rather aback) If I think of it, I will.

                               DADA
(suddenly) I'll shoot one in the beak for you. I just shot
one in the beak about ten minutes ago.

                               FISH
(still ferociously) They're animals! They don't respect the
conventions of war.

                              JERRY
(pointing to the front of the stage) I know. They get around
there on the footlights and shoot in at us.

                             GENERAL
Well, goodbye, Corporal, look me up after the war. (the fife
and drum strike up a march and follow the GENERAL and MR. FISH
from the stage)

                               DADA
Those fellows are going to get hit with a cannon ball first
thing they know ... Hm, I'm tired of looking here. I wish I
had a cup of coffee.

                              JERRY
What do you want coffee for? Coffee isn't good for you, Dada.

                               DADA
It keeps me awake.

                              JERRY
What do you want to stay awake for? That's right -- you got
to stay awake. So've I. (sternly) I got to make good. (into
the picture there now minces a YOUNG LADY WAR-WORKER, dressed
as young lady war-workers are usually dressed -- but with a faint
touch of jazz. Her name, by a remarkable coincidence, is DORIS)

                              DORIS
(heartily) Hello, Buddies. (at the sound of a voice DADA wheels
suddenly around to attention and presents arms)

DORIS
(to JERRY) Say, honestly did you ever see such a dumbbell.
(SHE looks closer) He must be going on to between seventy and
eighty years old if not older.

JERRY
He knows more than you give him credit for, don't you Dada?
(by this time DADA has perceived his error and turned away
thinking nobody noticed)

DORIS
I better introduce myself. I'm one of the girls in the Smile,
Grin and Laughter Service. The Smile, Grin and Laughter Service
is a new thing that has just been gotten up by a lot of patriotic
girls. It's considered a very good thing.

DADA
(turning around) Have you got any soup with you?

DORIS
No, we don't -- have any soup. Here's a package of good old
cigarettes -- for the boys.

JERRY
Don't give 'em to him. He thinks it's a dirty habit.

DORIS
Why?

JERRY
It was always considered sort of a dirty habit when he was a
man -- when he was a child.

DORIS
(running her words together for emphasis and narrowing her
eyes at DADA as if she had discovered a traitor in her midst)
You mean to say you don't think the girls in the Smiles, Grin
and Laughter Service ought to bring fags out?

DADA
(catching a word) Yes, I'm all fagged out.

DORIS
Say, honestly they oughtn't to let people like him in this war
at his age. He's liable to do something to lose it. He's
liable to forget which side he's on and there where would you be.

JERRY
That's all right. I keep telling him what it's about.

DORIS
Well, anyhow we girls in the Smiles, Grin and Laughter Service
are just like Buddies to the boys.

JERRY
(<u>resentfully</u>) Well, you haven't made me laugh yet.

DORIS
(<u>SHE'S memorized this</u>) A little laughter drives the battle
blues away and lets the peace grins and victory laughs come in.

DADA
(<u>hungry</u>) Did she say she had any soup?

JERRY
(<u>to DORIS</u>) Well, go on make me laugh, if you think you're so
funny.

DORIS
(<u>indignantly</u>) I don't think I'm funny.

JERRY
Then what did you say you thought you were for.

DORIS
Say, don't you understand the difference between a person
that's cheerful and a person that has a funny face or a wooden
leg or something?

JERRY
(<u>interrupting argumentatively</u>) Look here you say you're supposed
to be funny. Well -- go on and be funny then.

DORIS
Honestly, they got some of the most disagreeable people in
this war.

JERRY
I'm not disagreeable. I'm not disagreeable. I just said what
you said yourself. You said you belong to the -- thing --
whatever you belong to --

DORIS
Well, if I'd known that nobody knew what was the difference
between cheerful and funny I would have gone in some other
service.

JERRY
(<u>with great patience</u>) Listen, I -- know -- the difference
between funny and -- whatever it was. I know all those sort
of things. But what you said --

DORIS
(<u>still trying to explain the distinction</u>) Look at here. Would
you think it was funny if I started to -- oh, sing a funny song
or something?

JERRY

Well, let's see you do it.

DORIS

(indignantly) Say, I don't know any funny songs.

JERRY

Then what did you say you did for? Let's see you do it, you say you're so darn funny.

DORIS

I suppose you think I ought to stand on my head. (A MAN, who is either a military policeman or a Y.M.C.A. Secretary or perhaps a little of both comes in just in time to hear DORIS' last remark. HE bears a curious resemblance to MR. WARWICK, JERRY'S late secretary)

WARWICK

(to DORIS) You just try to get away with anything like that around here.

DADA

Has he got any soup?

WARWICK

No, but I've got orders to keep young girls out of the trenches.

DORIS

Listen, I'm one of the girls in the Smile, Grin and Laughter Service. It's a new thing that's just been gotten up.

JERRY

(helping DORIS out) They're sort of supposed to be funny. I've been laughing myself sick at some joke she told me. (to DORIS) What was that joke you just told me about -- about the two Jews? (HE winks at her -- then HE sees that WARWICK has fixed him with a malevolent eye) This -- this lodge she belongs to is supposed to be a very good thing.

WARWICK

My orders are that where there's fun there's liable to be something wrong.

JERRY

Well, then this girl is a -- a regular Madame de -- Madame de -- a regular -- Salome -- this girl's a regular Salome.

WARWICK

If I see anybody enjoying themselves I got orders to knock them out and drag them back behind the line. (here, mysteriously enough, DADA begins to dance stiffly on the fire-step and to sing in a cracked voice)

JERRY

What's the matter, Dada? (in the other trench two or three
BUZZARDS are observed to be gathering about a simple catapult.
To an accompaniment of cluck-clucking from farther back ANOTHER
BUZZARD staggers on with an enormous egg which is placed upon
the catapult. The catapult is fired and the shell -- the egg,
rather -- RISES VERY slowly into the air, soars across No-man's
land with an increasingly piercing siren sound and lands with
a loud explosion near DORIS AND JERRY. WARWICK with a frightened
cry rushes from the scene) (quickly) Egg Masks! (at this command
DORIS AND JERRY produce from their belts instruments which re-
semble lorgnettes but have nose-pieces instead of eye-glasses
attached. DADA does not hear the command but after a few sniffs
HE follows their example.) (When the danger is over JERRY AND
DORIS lower their masks. DADA, however, keeps his on)

DORIS

Honestly, I'm getting to be a nervous wreck. When a girl has
three fiancés killed in a war, one after another within six
months, it gets so it affects her nervous system.

JERRY

I should think you'd get in some other service.

DORIS

Oh, I believe in cheering the boys up, all right. I think it's
a good thing.

DADA

(lowering his mask cautiously) Did anybody get hit?

JERRY

(looking at his watch) No, but we got to go over the top in
a few minutes. (to DORIS) I got a wonderful scheme. Very
original. I been digging all day.

DORIS

I know. You've been mining underneath the Buzzards.

JERRY

Not unless you can talk about mining for worms.

DORIS

Worms.

JERRY

Yeah. Worms. Two big cans of worms.

DORIS

You going to fish?

JERRY

No. My idea is that if there's one thing a Buzzard can't resist it's a worm. That's what my scheme is. We're going to
throw over the worms before the attack.

DADA

(turning around) He's been digging worms. (sceptically) He thinks worms are going to win the war.

JERRY

Don't be such a wet blanket, Dada.

DADA

A wet blanket is just exactly what I feel like.

DORIS

Well, I'll say goodbye. Don't forget -- a little laughter drives the blues away and lets the peace [guns] grins and victory laughs come in. (DORIS goes out. JERRY rings a small dinner bell and the scene is immediately changed to one of activity. This is what occurs:

(Out of the dugouts crawl four or five soldiers, who brush off their clothes with whiskbrooms, take a last dab at their shoes, and clean their spectacles -- in fact make all the little preparations of a soldier before going "over the top." THE SOLDIERS are members of the last reserve -- and as such are too tall, too short, too fat or too lean, but the light of fierce determination is in their eyes.)

(Who should appear next but MR. (now Band Sergeant) STUTZ-MOZART, accompanied by THREE OR FOUR MUSICIANS armed with slide trombones, saxaphones, drums and other appropriate instruments.)

(A thunder storm begins)

JERRY

(addressing his men) Men -- everything has now gotten into the last ditch.

THE MEN

Hurray!

JERRY

After these worms are thrown over into the Buzzard trenches we will go over ourselves and change these Buzzards into -- into Birds of Paradise.

THE MEN

Hurray!

JERRY

All right! Altogether -- say it with worms! (THE SOLDIERS immediately fling the great cans of worms into the BUZZARD trenches. THE BUZZARDS -- there are about HALF A DOZEN OF THEM -- run for the worms with great cluckings.)

SGT. STUTZ-MOZART'S Orangotang band begins to play "The Dark
Town Strutters Ball" very softly -- THEY increase to fortissimo
as JERRY gives the order to GO OVER THE TOP.)

(The attack proceeds in this fashion. In the lead is JERRY,
followed by his intrepid MEN. Twenty feet behind comes Band
Sgt. STUTZ-MOZART with his Orangatang band. The orangotang
band proceeds in Jazz formation, THE MEMBERS stepping through
the Chicago, shaking their shoulders, playing catch with the
drumsticks and using the wind instruments for pipes of pan.)

(THE BUZZARDS, engrossed in the worms and taken by surprise,
retreat backward off the stage with a shrill uproar, followed
closely by JERRY AND HIS TROOPS. For a moment the stage is
deserted -- then there is the cheering sound of a fife and
drum and GENERAL COHEN marches on and proceeds jauntily in the
wake of the conflict.)

(It might be supposed here that we are to see no more of the
battle but there is no such disappointment in store. In fact
THE BUZZARDS have apparently been driven completely around the
backdrop for presently THEY appear on the American side and
retreat across the stage as before, pausing only to face to
the rear and fire. TWO of them fall dead.)

(The next phenomenon is the appearance of DADA in the wake of
the BUZZARDS. He has become a little confused as to sides --
in fact one might suppose him to be the BUZZARDS' rear guard,
for from time to time HE faces around and fires in the direction
of the pursuing American forces.)

(The American forces appear again -- JERRY is in the lead,
shouting "Dada, Dada! No! No! Dada," and MR. STUTZ-MOZART
and HIS BAND follow.)

(On reaching their own trench again, the surviving BUZZARDS
throw up their hands shouting "Birds of a Feather!" which,
as everyone knows, is the Buzzard term of submission.)

(The victory is now won -- and GENERAL COHEN with his fife and
drum arrives just as THE TROOPS are acclaiming JERRY, who stands
on top of No-man's land trying to look modest and unconcerned)

                    STUTZ-MOZART
(enthusiastically) Hooray! Victory! Hurray for Frost!

                    THE SOLDIERS
Hurray! Hurray!

                    JERRY
(modestly) It wasn't so much me that won the war as it was the
worms! (a commotion in the crowd. A SOLDIER pushes his way
through)

THE SOLDIER
(saluting) We have captured a dangerous looking prisoner, sir.
(THE PRISONER is brought in with his hands tied behind his back
and a great cloth over his face. When the cloth is removed the
unfortunate DADA is disclosed. HE is released)

GENERAL COHEN
Corporal Frost, you've made good. Your place is in the White
House.

JERRY
I've tried to make good. I knew I had it in me.

ALL
Hooray! Strike up the band! Frost for re-election! (THE BAND
begins to play and there is a gorgeous and patriotic tableau
with the modest JERRY in the Center.) (Then suddenly there ENTERS
a discordant note. A diminutive taxi-cab has driven on to the
American side of the stage. It contains TWO PEOPLE, A MAN AND
A WOMAN -- otherwise JOSEPH FISH and our old friend CHARLOTTE.
The taxi-cab bears a sign which reads "Battlefield Tours."
CHARLOTTE is wearing the traditional blue veil of the tourist
while FISH carries a map and has a pair of enormous field glasses
slung at his side.) (As if perceiving the inappropriateness
of this apparition the sound of the victory music dies away
and the heads of the late COMBATANTS turn toward THE TOURISTS
who have disembarked from the taxi-cab and are inspecting the
American trench)

CHARLOTTE
(arranging her veil) What's this?

FISH
This is the -- this is the -- this is where they had some
battle or something.

CHARLOTTE
(staring around in disapproval) Hm! Looks it! (SHE sniffs)
Nitro-glycerine -- I can smell that stuff up here. (at this
remark JERRY, across the stage, is seen to start) Say, did you
ever see such hotels as they've got on these Buzzard Islands?

FISH
They're robbers.

CHARLOTTE
That's what they are. Robbers -- they're robbers. (THEIR
VOICES die away as THEY become involved in sympathethic
agreement)

                              JERRY
(to the SOLDIERS)   I wish to state that I've changed my mind
completely around.   I don't want to be President.   I wouldn't
take it if I was elected to it in a golden plate.

                         [GENERAL COHEN
What do you want then, Corporal?

                              JERRY
(confidentially)   Well, then I just don't want to be always
picked on all the time.

                           GENERAL
Hm!   I don't know whether I can manage that!

                              JERRY
(in a pleading voice, after a glance over at CHARLOTTE)
Everybody's always picking on me all the time.   I just want
to do what I want.   (passionately)   I just want to be left
alone.   Will you try to fix it?   Will you try to fix it?

                              ALL
Yes!   Yes!   (amid cheers and with the sympathetic eyes of
EVERYONE -- except, of course, CHARLOTTE AND JOSEPH FISH --
fixed upon JERRY]

                   THE CURTAIN DESCENDS

Nixon's Apollo Theatre

Telephone—Marine 3146

The Nixon Apollo Theatre Company...............Lessees
FRED G. NIXON-NIRDLINGER.....Pres. & Gen'l Mgr.
Guy S. Burley ....Business Manager
Harold Manypenny }
Clarence D. Stewart } ....Treasurers
Walter Raymond ....Stage Manager
Charles G. Miller ....Electrician
James J. Brown.......................... Advertising Agent
C. B. Riley.......................................Properties

One Week Commencing Monday, November 19, 1923

Mats. Wednesday and Saturday

SAM H. HARRIS Presents

Ernest Truex

in

F. SCOTT FITZGERALD'S Comedy

The Vegetable

(From President to Postman)

Staged by Sam Forrest

The characters concerned in the disclosure are:
Jerry Frost
(The Vegetable himself).................Ernest Truex
Charlit
(His wife, who means practically no good)
Minna Gombel
Dada
(Jerry's father and a great thinker. He will
never see eighty-eight again)..David Higgins
Doris
(Charlotte's sister, who learned about life
from the silver screen).........Ruth Hammond
Mr. Snookes (or Snukes)
(An astounding product of our constitution)
Malcolm Williams
Joseph Fish
(An Idaho sheik, beloved of Doris)
Donald MacDonald
Major General Pushing, U. S. A.
(You will hear more of him later)..Walter Walker
Chief Justice Fossile
(Of the Supreme Court. He needs no intro-
duction) ....Harry Hammill
Mr. Jones
(Highly recommended by the King of Eng-
land) ....Harold de Becker

Mr. Stutz-Mozart
(The venerable Jazz King).................Luis Alberni
A Chauffeur
(Who is also a herald).......................H. H. Gibson
A Newsboy
(He will speak for himself)............Barney Warren
A Postman
(Just a common postman)..William H. Pendergast
Mr. McSullivan
(The well-known politician)....William H. Malone
Also a Drummer and a Fifer
Their real names are..Walter Millar, Leslie Millar
And finally there are some Senators
In private life they are known as
Robert Mack, Harry Ford, Frank Bronson,
John Paul, Horace Grey, Miller Cushman

THE FIRST ACT
is the living room in the Frosts' house. It was not
designed by Elsie de Wolf. It just happened.
But when you come to

THE SECOND ACT
you will be glad to learn that we're now on the
lawn of the White House—yes, the Executive Mansion itself, at Washington, D. C.
However, the pace is pretty fast there, so in

THE THIRD ACT
(Which occurs two weeks after the first) we return
to the dear little love nest of the Frost family.

Howard Hull Gibson............................Stage Manager
Settings designed by Clark Robinson.
Built by McDonald and painted by Roth &
Teichner.
Costumes designed by Gilbert Adrian.
Executed by Brooks Mahieu Theatrical Costumers.
Shoes by I. Miller.
Wigs by Hepner.

Musical Program Week of November 19, 1923
Music during the intermissions by Albert C.
Goebel's Apollo Theatre Orchestra, under the direc-
tion of John H. Haines.
Overture
Chinese March—"Kwang Hsu".......................Lincke
Intermission Act I
Grand Selection from the Opera "Pagliacci"
Leoncavallo
Fox Trot—"Just One More Kiss".................Berger
Intermission Act II
Airs from the Musical Success, "The Clinging
Vine" ....Levey
Waltz—"A Kiss in the Dark".......................Herbert
Exit March—"I've Got a Song for Sale".........Nelson

Appendix II

This section contains two consecutive sets of "corrections and addenda" made by Fitzgerald for the final acting script while the play was in rehearsal during the late summer of 1923. The performance version involved relatively minor alterations of the original published book; and Fitzgerald's page references make these final revisions easy to follow. Here, too, the original manuscript (Princeton University Library) has been transcribed without any alterations or corrections, except that Fitzgerald's own deletions are shown in brackets. The second set of changes refers to the first set as well as to the printed book.

CHANGES AND ADDENDA TO "THE VEGETABLE"

(Numbers refer to pages of the printed book)

Act I

P. 11   Insert after the words "so he went away":

> The bell rings again, [and] Jerry answers it with alacrity
> and in steps a weary, night-bound postman who says "Good
> Evening" and hands Jerry a lone, uninteresting letter,
> probably an advertisement. Jerry looks at the postman
> with rising interest.

JERRY.   Say, you're kinda late, arn't you?

THE POSTMAN.   Yeah. We're short of men. I hada do two
men's work today.

JERRY.   You get a lot of exercise on that job, don't
you? Lot of walking?

THE POSTMAN.   Yeah.

JERRY.   That's what I like about it. You get a lot of
exercise.

THE POSTMAN.   You in the service?

JERRY.   No-o-o. I got a desk job down at the railroad.
Say, that's a pretty suit they make you wear.

THE POSTMAN.   Kinda nifty, ain't it.

(The postman has been looking admiringly about the room,
obviously in admiration of the tasty decorations)

THE POSTMAN.   Say, that's a fine bunch of photos you
got on them walls.

(Jerry hasn't thought of the photos for a long time but in
the light of the postman's approval they begin to assume
value in his eyes.)

JERRY.   (smugly) I always thought they were sort of
artistic

THE POSTMAN.   They must of cost you a lot of money

JERRY.   Yeah, they cost a lot to have 'em taken.

THE POSTMAN.   Kinda artistic having 'em all around.

JERRY.   Well, that's the idea I had. And then if I
          forget how anybody looks or anything I can just
          look up on the wall.

(The postman has now advanced into the room and is inspecting the art gallery.)

JERRY.   This one's my father. He lives with us.

THE POSTMAN.   Old fella, eh?

JERRY.   (proudly) He was born in 1834.

THE POSTMAN.   (innocently) A.D. or B.C.?

JERRY.   (quite seriously) A.D.

THE POSTMAN.   (flabbergasted) Well, what do you know
                about that? (He stares again at the
                picture)

JERRY.   He's a great thinker. He's thought a lot of
          things out.

(The postman nods comprehendingly and they move on to the
next picture.)

JERRY.   This is my wife here. This is the way she used
          to be when we got married, and (without malice)
          this is the way she is now.

(The postman nods his head appraisingly, looking from one
picture to the other.)

JERRY.   And this is her sister Doris. (With any en-
          couragement he would go around the whole gal-
          lery, but the postman, still nodding in approval,
          moves toward the door. Jerry's face falls.)

THE POSTMAN.   Well, I got to be going. If you ever get
                tired of your desk [want a] job [as a
                carrier] just let me know.

(They both smile)

JERRY.   Drop in again, will you?

THE POSTMAN.   Sure I will. Good night.

      He goes out.

P. 11.   Cut Charlotte's speech beginning "I thought" ect.
         and substitute the following.

    CHARLOTTE.   Who was that you were talking too?

    JERRY.   Oh, that was just the postman.

    CHARLOTTE.   Havn't you got anything better to do
    than talk to the postman?

    JERRY.   Now listen here, Charlit --

    CHARLOTTE.   Next think you'll be asking the milkman to
    come into breakfast. (scornfully) a
    common postman.

    JERRY.   (indignantly) Common? Why, Charlit, he was one
    of the -- one of the healthiest men I ever saw
    in my life.

    CHARLOTTE.   I should think you'd have something better
    to do than talk to the postman. A big,
    strong man like you. I thought you were go-
    ing to the Republican Convention down at the
    Auditorium.

P. 17   Add this to Charlotte's first speech:

(She begins to look indignantly through a magazine) Well,
just listen here what I found in this magazine that you
are. Just listen here. Wait a minute now--just--wait--
one--minute. (she reads) "Any man who doesn't want to
get on in the world and make a million dollars hasn't got
as much to him as a a good dog has -- he's nothing more or
less than a vegetable." That's what you are, see? It
says so right here.

(For a moment Jerry considers this gloomily)

p. 29.   Cut the first two sentences of Doris' last speech.

p. 55   Jerry's final speech should be:

    "I'll -- I'll ask my wife"

Three million then--but look at here, Honorable Snooks,
I got to save some for a war I got [under consideration]
ordered. I don't want to seem tight, but--.

P. 87   Substitute for Jerry's first speech.

"Well, I don't like to beat you down but--" (he sees
Snooks shrugging his shoulders and adds hastily:) "Four
million."

Pps 91-94   See book for cuts.

P. 105   Cut the words "Buffalo Bill and".
                         or
           "Old King Brady" or "Nick Carter"
                         or
           "The Liberty Boys of Seventy-six"

P. 108   Insert before Pushings first speech.

     JERRY   --You're just kidding, arn't you general? The
               General's a great kidder. Ha-ha.

           (His laughter fades as the General continues)

P. 110   See book for speech cut.

Charlottes last speech in Act II.

"So you've turned out to be a drunkard too, you poor,
weak, miserable failure."